Andrew Hutchinson is
and currently lives
Rohypnol won the Victo
Award for Best Unpubli ....script. He is
currently working on his second novel.
www.myspace.com/hutchinsona

ANDREW HUTCHINSON

Rohypnol _{AH}

VINTAGE BOOKS

Australia

A Vintage Book
Published by Random House Australia Pty Ltd
Level 3, 100 Pacific Highway, North Sydney, NSW 2060
www.randomhouse.com.au

Sydney   New York   Toronto
London   Auckland   Johannesburg

National Library of Australia
Cataloguing-in-Publication Entry

Hutchinson, Andrew, 1979–.
Rohypnol.

ISBN 978 1 74166 822 3.

I. Title.

A823.4

Cover photograph by Kateryna Govorushchenko
Cover design by Mathematics
Typeset in Egyptienne F by Midland Typesetters, Australia
Printed and bound by Griffin Press, South Australia

10 9 8 7 6 5 4 3 2 1

Rohypnol

Troy fucked up. He broke the rules, and now he's in the passenger seat beside me, his huge steroid-fuelled body hunched over the dashboard. The edges of his bleached white hair are gathered together with sweat. His cheeks move in and out, quick, like he's biting on his own teeth.

And we're waiting, sitting in Thorley's red two-door sports car, looking out along a still street. Silent in the early morning. The houses, lined off along either side of the road ahead of us, brick fences and letterboxes. Tidy, green-grass gardens with pebble-stone paths. Leaves that float in swirls, like paper snowflakes in the early morning air. It's a rich area, all double-storey places with high arch windows and balconies and double-garages with automatic doors. Maybe I would have wanted to live here once.

Troy is panicked, pushing his palms together and swallowing too often.

'I can't go to jail,' he says. Sounds like he's

out of breath. Like he's about to cry. 'You've got to help me.'

Troy's muscles are too big. He's been upping his steroids, boosting the testosterone. His veins are pushed to the surface, blue lines curling along his arms. He's been using for almost two years, taking him from a skinny nothing to a giant. I've wanted to ask him if the steroids make his balls shrink, but some things you just don't. Especially not of users who can pop your skull with their grip. Mention to Troy how you had to wait some place and he'll tell you how many kilos he can lift.

'What do you think?' he asks.

'Shut up,' I tell him.

Troy broke the rules and ended up calling me at 4 am, telling me how he could taste blood that wasn't his. How his room was covered in it. He took some girl home from a nightclub. Troy talked to her and kissed her neck and held her hand while she drank drinks with her friends, and then he took her back to his place. But he fucked up because he knew them. They know him. And they can identify him. Tall. Spiky, bleached hair. Built like the Hulk. So we're watching the houses, waiting for one of the friends to come out, walk to school. We're waiting so we can tell her to keep her mouth shut.

Fact: If she talks we are fucked.

'I'm not . . . We were just fucking around.'

Troy's talking too fast, telling me stories he's heard about prison. Prisoners raping guys with broken broom handles. Prisoners dropping heavy weights on a guy's crotch. A gang of prisoners pouring boiling water on a rapist's cock, melting everything together.

'It wasn't supposed to happen.' Troy, using his innocent face, looks to me, his eyes clouded with tears. 'I mean – '

'Shut up. You broke the fucking rules. Let's just get this shit done.' In my stomach I can feel the panic setting in, that sick, dark feeling. I'm thinking of courtroom scenes on news shows, police questioning. Troy shuts his eyes tight, buries his face into his hands. I'm thinking of my parents, looking down on me. The family fuck-up. 'Where is this girl? Do you even remember what she looks like?'

'Yes.' Troy sounds defeated, upset, takes his hands from his face to speak.

'What was her name?'

'I forget the fucking name. She lives here.'

'Who told you she lives here?' I yell, turn to stare right at him.

'This is where we dropped her off in the taxi,' Troy yells back at me, breathing hard. His big chest expanding and falling. 'I think.'

'You fucking think?'

'I don't know, not for sure.' Troy blinks hard, puts his hands up onto the dashboard, his eyes shifting away from me, looks ahead through the windscreen. 'Wait,' he says, pointing. 'Wait, that's her.'

The girl walks out to the footpath, three houses up from where we're parked, skips to avoid a crack in the concrete, walks away from us. She has her school dress on, white socks to her knees. Her dark hair is tied up, streaks of white-blonde highlights. She carries her bag at her side, the strap across her chest.

'Fuck,' Troy says quietly, more to himself than me.

I start the engine, accelerate the car up ahead of her, pull into the gutter, turn to look at Troy, my elbow rested on the steering wheel.

'We have to do this quickly, right? Straight up on her, no fucking around, get her in the car and we're gone, yeah?'

Troy nods, his eyes closed tight, his bottom lip sucked in.

'Open your eyes,' I tell him, point at his face. 'No fucking around,' I repeat, and I push the door open.

And we are both out and up in her face on the footpath, car doors swinging behind us. The girl rolls her eyes up to meet mine, scans to Troy then back to me. She smiles with her mouth closed, her head tilted slightly. The girl is Aleesa Desca. She narrows her eyes when she sees me.

That sick feeling, like being choked from the inside.

Troy looks to me, unsure what to say.

'We have to talk,' I tell her.

'What do we have to talk about?' She stands tall, unafraid. Lifts the heel of one foot.

'Just get in the car.'

'And you,' she rolls her eyes to Troy. 'You went home with April, huh?'

Troy says nothing, his eyes wide, looks to me.

'How was she?'

Troy grabs her arm suddenly, pushes her towards the open car door, hard enough to make her jolt as she goes.

'What? What the fuck are you doing?' Aleesa says, her teeth close to Troy's ear.

He stuffs her into the back seat and we get in, slam the doors shut, accelerate along the street.

Aleesa, a sudden emergency in her voice, she's saying: 'You fucking idiots, what do you want? What's happened?'

'Aleesa, shut the fuck up.' I talk over my shoulder as I drive, Troy breathing hard beside me. 'We need you to do something.'

I catch her eye in the mirror. She stares, impatient, demanding. Push the car faster along the empty street. She raises one eyebrow when she talks.

'What have you guys – '

'We need to make it clear that you did not see this guy,' I say, pointing to Troy. 'You did not see him at any point last night.'

'Fuck,' Troy growls under his breath, rubs at his forehead.

Aleesa looks at him, at the panic on his face.

The sweat on the back of his neck. The fear in his voice. She flicks her head back quick, her eyes open wide.

'What's happened to April?' she says.

Troy grips at his seatbelt, his knuckles white.

'If you guys have done anything – '

'Aleesa, for your sake you didn't see him, right?' I say.

'Fuck. Off.' Aleesa stares me down in the mirror, lifts her chin as she speaks. 'You stupid fucks can't intimidate me. If anything's happened I'll go straight to the cops.' She leans closer to the front seat to make sure we hear. Every. Word. 'I'll tell them everything. Everyone knows about your rape squad.'

Troy is grinding his teeth, loud enough for me to hear it, the knuckles of his clenched fist getting whiter. Shaking. Strangling the seatbelt. Any moment, he's going to tear this car apart. He looks to me. I know what's about to happen. Aleesa's dark eyes stare hard at mine in the mirror.

'You're going to regret that,' I tell her.

As therapy they make me write. Some doctor at some college in America discovered that people who have gone through a traumatic experience, like a war or a murder in the family, they have a faster mental recovery time if they write everything down. Like facing up to your demons.

Some Vietnam veteran wrote about soldiers going crazy with their rifles, emptying hundreds of rounds into a water buffalo in the rice fields of Saigon. I read that story. Another guy wrote about an orangutan that lived in the trees near their base camp and would come down and steal their food at night. They write this, these veterans, and it's a release for them. Release from years of forced assimilation into nine-to-five society after they've put bullets into the faces of strangers. Apparently, writing helps them with this. Helps them sleep with empty thoughts.

And now they are trying this on criminals, mostly young guys who've 'lost their way'. Maybe if they make me write this, maybe I'll be normal again. Fit into place. Maybe I won't have to go out and rape their daughters any more. This is the logic.

So I'm writing this for them. A requirement. I'm writing about everything. How everything went wrong. My parents, paying good money for my therapy, I want them to read this. I want them to know all of it. But most of all, I want them to know that this – the therapy, the police, the court trials – I want everyone to know that this won't change a thing. The psychologist, the concerned families, the people who know better – I want them all to read this and know I will not change.

Fact: I am a bad person.

I've seen and done things you'd be afraid to even think about. I've watched it happen and done nothing to stop it. And I don't feel one bit bad about it.

The innocent victims.

The girls we've fucked up for future relationships.

The parents holding hands to get through their grief.

I don't lie awake at night thinking about it. I don't regret my actions.

I don't want to change.

In fact, I'll make sure I don't change just to fuck that college genius in the ass. All those hardened war veterans bawling their eyes out on his leather couch. This will not change me. I want you to read this, all of it, and know as you

8

turn the pages, sitting in bed, reading lamp shining out across your silent room, know that I have not learned my lesson. I have not mended my ways.

I am a bad person. Some things will not change, no matter how hard you try.

And fuck it, I don't want them to.

Thorley has short dark hair that is consistently messed up every day. A geeky kind of guy, quiet, never says much in class. His first name is something only rich people would give their kid, like Giles or Pierre. His favourite character from *The Simpsons* is Gil, the depressed businessman. He says *Ghost Dog* is the best film he has ever seen. Thorley has light-blue eyes and thin lips. Think Ethan Hawke, but not as pretty. One time I found him on the floor of his house, naked, sharpening a pin.

I met Thorley at school. But before that my family got rich. Dad was an I.T. guy, one of the first internet experts telling people how one day everyone would own a computer. My dad, he made his fortune on the back of the Y2K scare. Dad worked for big companies, banks, updating lines of code to make sure that when the world came to an end, when technology shut down and society dipped into chaos, when that happened, their credit card records would be safe. By the time the Y2K scare had worn off we were rich.

'Well off' is how my mum describes it.

It happened like this: I fucked up in school on a regular basis, I got expelled and my dad sent me to a private school, told me: 'You better sort yourself out.' My parents figured the best education money could buy might get me back in line. On the right path. Also, Mum liked the colours of the uniform, the pictures of the kids in the brochure.

Then there I was, among old-style buildings carved out of concrete blocks. Mothers wearing oversized sunglasses and spotted scarves. Fifteen-year-old kids discussing politics. Guys with bleached teeth and solarium tans. Everything about the place reeked of 'social status'. Everything shined, looked like an American movie. The sprinkler stuttering across the cropped grass in the morning. The shining sports cars in the parking lot. Everything was dripping with money.

Here, there are two kinds of people: those who want to be like their parents and those who don't. Me, I wanted to burn the place down. Watch the roof beams collapse and shatter into burning sparks in the night.

This is how it started.

I talked to no-one at that fucking school for three months. Three months, until Thorley said something to me in a chemistry class. Three months, and Thorley had noticed me looking at the chemistry teacher in her white lab coat with her black underwear showing under the jittering fluorescent lights. Her hands on the test tubes. Her tits on the back of my shoulder as she leaned over to correct my calculations. Thorley had seen this.

The chemistry teacher and the maths teacher were married. Honestly, I have no idea what her first name was. Her last name was Arthur, by marriage to Mr John Arthur. I remember his name. Lodged in my memory like a splinter of glass under my skin.

Thorley had seen me looking at her, and he walked over to my table, stood in front of me with a smile. He told me I could have her, Mrs Arthur. Apparently, some of the other guys already had.

'She's easy,' Thorley told me.

But this would not have happened if Mr John Arthur hadn't fucked up. Mr Arthur, he'd decided to seek me out every day.

'Still dealing?' he'd ask. 'Still using?' he'd say, telling me how he knew about my past dealing drugs at my old school. He'd be standing over me, his comb-over hair blowing up and away from his shining bald head in the sunlight, and Mr John Arthur would say: 'Heard you broke a kid's fingers with a hammer at your old school.' A story that always sounds much worse if you weren't there to see it. 'You're a tough guy, aren't you? We don't tolerate bullies around here.'

One time he grabbed my arm, said: 'Don't fuck with me,' right up in my ear. As if saying 'fuck' would make me realise he meant business.

In hindsight, I'm sure Mr John Arthur thought he was doing me a favour, trying to scare me into a straight line. I know how it works. But Mr John Arthur pissed me off on two counts.

One, he made me feel weak and pathetic in front of those fucking rich kids. Two, he became the personification of everything I hated about that school. That feeling that they wanted to clean the place after seeing me in it. My shitty little life eroding before me. And with every word he spoke, Mr John Arthur became, in my mind, the prime supporter of the judgemental stares and whispers as I walked through the corridors.

It's an issue of equality. If someone burns you, you should do the same to them.

Thorley sits down next to me at lunchtime, tells me where Mrs Arthur goes on Fridays after work, the same European-themed pub every week. Tiny flags of the world hanging above the bar. Original Guinness advertisements on the walls. She meets friends and they dance to retro music, reminds them of their lives before they became who they are. Thorley tells me he's seen her there. He's followed her before. I ask if he's been with her, but Thorley never answers direct questions like this.

'Ironically,' Thorley says, 'to fuck the chemistry teacher you will have to learn about chemistry.'

Thorley's parents live in France. His dad is the head of some security company, worked with government agencies as a consultant. He has a picture of his dad with Kofi Annan, and when Thorley shows me this he tells me how when he was younger he always thought he was Morgan Freeman.

Thorley's dad transferred to Paris last year, so they bought Thorley a million-dollar apartment in the Melbourne CBD and a red car with shining mag wheels and his parents left. At Christmas they come back for four weeks, the rest of the time Thorley is lord of the manor. His parents left him with a thirty-thousand-dollar credit card and a kiss on the cheek, and they were gone.

Thorley is eighteen, a year older than the rest of us. He got kept back a grade because he got a gun held to his head when he was a kid. He was in an armed hold-up at a bank, Thorley and his mother. Apparently, they taped his hands to his face and they did something to his Mum and he got a year off school.

To get to Thorley's apartment you pass through glass security doors, then a shining black-tiled hall, past an art installation, up an elevator and home. The apartment is neat and calculated. On the table by the windows there's a collection of test tubes and Bunsen burner type devices, bubbling and working in the sunlight. This is Thorley's drug lab. His science work. He tells me he is against anything that has to be injected. Too extreme, he says.

'Benzodiazepine,' Thorley says, holding up a small plastic bag. 'This is what we will be working with for today's experiment.'

Everything starts off small. A melanoma on your skin. A loose bolt on the carnival ride. The smallest thing can start a disaster. Just a few words can fuck everything up. It's how it ends that people can't shake from their memory.

Benzodiazepine. Rohypnol. Ketamine. Before Thorley I had no idea about these things. Look it up on the internet, Rohypnol, and a thousand web pages will come up. Date rape. GHB is another one.

It works like this:

Rohypnol is a benzodiazepine, a central nervous system depressant. Imagine Valium times ten. It's manufactured to treat severe sleep disorders. Rohypnol can be taken orally, snorted or injected. It's sometimes used by ravers to stop post-high depression. Rohypnol will take effect within twenty minutes. Rohypnol will dissolve clear in liquid. In the mid-nineties the drug became so well known as a date-rape drug that its manufacturer started selling a new version which turns blue in liquid. This is why you should never trust anyone offering you a blue drink. The effects of Rohypnol can last for up to twelve hours. It will stay in your system for seventy-two hours.

Rohypnol is also amazingly cheap.

After twenty minutes you will feel drunk, but more than normal. Some people trip out, hallucinate. You'll have trouble talking clearly, like your mouth is dry but too moist at the same time. Your tongue won't keep up with your mind. Then comes the in and out feeling, taking in where you are, reprocessing reality, then out again. Your motor skills fail. Try making a Vulcan 'V' with your fingers and you'll fall over. Try tying your shoelaces, your necktie. You might black out depending on how much you've had, but you'll come back in again like nothing happened. This is when you are open to suggestion.

Rohypnol causes retrograde amnesia, meaning you will not remember what happens next. Most people are still active, still making noise, moving, but their powers are greatly hindered. Some people even seem to enjoy the sudden sex with strangers, go along with the whole deal. Like they instinctively register a pattern of activity which, to them, is sex. In their mind, they are with their boyfriend or husband. Mostly, these are the girls who have had a lot of sex in their time. At least, that's our theory. Whoever they are, they are most definitely not in reality. To them, it isn't happening. In a way, it isn't.

It's as if the real world shuts off, suddenly becomes a film. A film you star in but will never see.

And in the morning you will have a headache, but it will just feel like a bad hangover. As hard as you try, your recollection will almost certainly be blank. If done right, there will be no indication that anything ever happened other than a normal Saturday night. A section of your life rubbed out. Like the conscience of a criminal who does not care.

A blank.

Thorley buys two bottles of Corona and we choose a table in the darker corner of the pub, away from the main crowd gathered around the bar. It's early, so there are only a few people, mostly guys in business shirts, their ties loosened off and hanging from their necks, playing pool and flirting with the bar chick.

'She's hot,' I tell Thorley, point to the bar girl. 'American accent, I think.'

Thorley looks over. 'She's okay. You can do better than that, though.'

'Yeah, thanks man,' I laugh. 'She'd have so many fucking guys trying to get into her pants each night we wouldn't stand a chance anyway.'

Thorley smiles. 'You can have anyone you want now,' he says, drinks his beer, stares out at the crowd. 'You could take her home any night you want.' Thorley rocks on his chair, looks all around the room. 'She'll be here soon. Always is.'

'How many times have you watched her?'

'You know, I've never thought to use her against Mr Arthur,' Thorley says, turns back around, looks at me. 'That's fucking great, man.' And he holds his beer up, tilts it towards me.

'So how does this work?' I ask.

'We usually have a couple of the other guys with us so we can keep a watch out for each other, but fuck it, we'll be fine in this place.'

'And she won't remember anything?'

Thorley smiles, shadows from the lights above across his face. 'Never happened before,' he says.

'But she could, like, when she sees us again, maybe she'd have deja vu or some shit and she might piece it together. Maybe?'

'Yeah,' Thorley shrugs. 'Maybe.'

I narrow my eyes at him. 'You'd be fucked if you got caught doing this.'

Thorley smiles again, leans back, staring out at the crowd. Some guys, already drunk, trying to get the bar chick to talk to them. They laugh and point at each other when she walks away from them, check out her ass as she bends to get a bottle of something for another customer.

'She is pretty,' Thorley says, without taking his eyes off her.

'How many other guys do this with you?' I ask.

'Only a couple. Don't want too many.' Thorley keeps staring over at the bar girl. Short blonde hair, tied up. Black sleeveless T-shirt. 'So you got expelled?' he asks, looks to me.

I nod my head.

'What'd you do?' Thorley says, settles into his seat for the story.

'I fucked up, that's what I did.'

'Heard you were dealing?'

I put my head down, try to ignore the question.

'You still dealing?' Thorley asks, staring at me.

'No.' Keep facing down, look at the marks and scratches across the surface of the table.

Thorley laughs. 'So what happened?' he continues.

I face up to him, force a smile.

'Fuck people,' he says. 'Fuck them before they fuck you, that's my theory. Get the first punch in.'

Thorley clinks his bottle against mine and I laugh, smile at this logic.

Fuck people.

'Oh, also, do you have a problem with other guys seeing you naked?' Thorley asks, looking back out to the crowd, tips his Corona bottle towards his mouth.

'Don't think so,' I tell him.

Thorley puts his bottle down onto the table, looks calm, relaxed.

'There she is,' he says, straightening his back and stretching his neck up, his chin in the air, nods his head in the direction of Mrs Arthur, who has just walked through the door. Smiling. A flower in her hair. Black dress, thin straps over her shoulders. Thorley gets back down close to the table, leans across to speak to me.

'Three drinks,' he says, holds up three fingers. 'We let her have three drinks, then we do this. You'll keep a look out, and when she gets her fourth I'll pretend like I was bumped and hit her drink.' Thorley shows me a re-sealable bag, powder in the bottom corner of it. 'I've ground it up to make it dissolve faster.'

Thorley stuffs the bag back into his pocket, sucks down what's left of his beer. His eyes locked onto mine.

'You cool?' he asks.

'Yeah.'

'You sure?'

I think of Mr John Arthur standing over me. Smiling. 'Let's fucking do this.'

Thorley looks back over his shoulder at Mrs Arthur, standing by the bar, laughing with her friends. Turns his head back to face me, looks down at the table between us.

'We are gonna fuck her so bad,' he says, smiling.

Holds a hand out for me to give him a low five.

In class, Thorley can barely hold back laughter, his mouth filling with air, snorting back out his nose, and when I look at the excitement in his eyes I think to myself: *I am looking at a monster*. My heart feels like I have the foresight of a great tragedy.

Imagine going back in time and being there in the moments before the first plane smashed through the World Trade Center. Watching it unfold and being powerless to stop it. You know it's going to happen, but you pray that it's not. That this is not real.

Mr John Arthur, he's at the front of the room, shifting books and opening folders. He sees a yellow envelope, his name written in thick black letters. Mr John Arthur flips open the package, slides out a pile of photographs.

Any moment now, I'll realise this isn't happening. Any moment, I'm dead.

My arms shaking, my legs.

Feels like a balloon is being blown up inside my body, getting bigger and bigger, choking me up.

In front of his eyes, Mr John Arthur is looking at a photo of his wife dancing with another man, the stranger's face out of shot. His wife looking drunk in the next photo, smiling. The man with his hand on her back, just above her ass. His wife at a hotel, in a gold-coloured lobby, leaning into the stranger. His wife in her bra, a black-lace, see-through type, her nipples hard. That body he knows so well. His wife bent over, her matching black g-string in the poor yellow lighting of the hotel room. His wife with her tongue touching the skin of the stranger. His wife naked, touching her own breasts, her back arched up. The stranger fucking her, taking her from behind on the bed. The stranger, his face always out of frame, with his fingers inside her as she lies on her back.

Mr John Arthur is seeing memories. The time they met. Their first kiss. His heart slowly suffocating.

In his memories he watches her sleeping, how beautiful she looks. How her eyes lie waiting for him behind her hair, which plays across her face in the breeze. Mr John Arthur is slow-dancing with her on the carpet of their lounge room. These are memories of the wife he loves.

And in front of his eyes he sees her, porn-star pose. A penis intruding on a shot of her face, her eyes half-closed, dribbles of semen shining on her lips, mixing with her make-up. A hand smearing them together across her cheek. The woman he loves.

Mr John Arthur looks around the classroom, his eyes blaming everybody through a fine layer of tears. He can't speak. He wants to grind his teeth to dust and spit fire across the halls. He wants to smash the faces of the hundreds of students, shatter bone and taste blood.

Mr John Arthur, he stands, places the pictures back into the envelope, walks out, being careful not to slam the door behind him. The air feels thick all around. No-one talks. Thorley bites at the edge of his hand, where his thumb connects, chugging short bursts of laughter under his breath.

Imagine the plane has just hit. Shards of glass shattered, raining down on the streets below.

People running and screaming, the noise rising.

And rising.

As the world crumbles around me.

Smashing to the ground.

The dust-cloud growing, rolling towards me, hard debris flicking against my skin as it takes over everything.

Then it stops.

Reality settles back to the bottom of my brain. The classroom is silent, everyone looking at each other vacantly, shaking their heads. Voices.

Thorley leans over, writes 'FUCK' on the cover of the notebook in front of me. I scribble over it with my pen, concentrate on blacking it out, make sure there are no gaps where you can see any trace of the word. Push the pen hard into the cardboard, dent it in. Rip it. Push right through it.

To me, there are points in life where you choose who you are. Follow that guy who cut you off in traffic. Get ready to swing a punch during an argument with your wife. Go to your boss's house, knock on his door, wait for him with a wrench in your fist. You either cross the line, or you don't.

But once you have gone over that line, once you've gone that step too far, you can never go back to life as it once was.

This is how everything went wrong.

The New Punk is about intelligence. It's about knowing your shit enough to justify not giving a shit any more. It's about understanding that the world will fuck you and there is not one thing you can do about it.

The New Punk is about raiding the twentieth century to make something new. There are no new ideas, no new music or films. Mash up songs. Remake classics. Cover versions. Re-living your life through these moments in pop culture, which have raised and educated you more than any person ever did. Like strangers you know very well.

The New Punk is not about religion, people going to churches every week to pray to be forgiven, take away a clean slate, come back and do the same again next Sunday. Watching people justify their lives by a rule book so they'll qualify for something that might happen when they die. Restricting their one life in the hope of something better when it's over. But there may be no better than this. Maybe this is all there is.

The New Punk is about living your fucking life.

No restrictions. No rule book. You are living today, fuck the consequences of tomorrow. There is no hindsight when your brain disconnects.

The New Punk is about taking control. Seeing what you want and taking it, no matter the cost. Isn't that what years of Hollywood has taught us? Talk shows and current affairs programs and stories of inspiration saying you can't wait for life. Saying take it now. It's about living, fuck who you think you are, fuck what anyone else will do. Fuck the reaction. Your life could end at any moment. There will be no reason to it, no justice. When it's your turn, you will go. So fuck everyone else, your life is about you, right now.

Fuck people.

The New Punk is about equality. If someone fucks with you, you need to fuck with them. It's about revenge. About never forgetting. Forgiveness can come when the playing field is levelled. If someone burns you, you take it back to them. But harder. If someone steals your lunch, you steal his wallet. If someone breaks your pencil, you break his fingers. If someone fucks your girlfriend, you fuck his mother. You wait outside her house with a razor blade in your fist. You take her down, stomp on her face, leave her bleeding on the concrete.

The New Punk is not about remorse.

The New Punk is not about moving towards your future. It is about your life right now, impatiently standing still.

It was partly curiosity and partly some feeling of debt to Thorley that led to me joining their road trip. And there we are, humming along the freeway in the morning light, past the empty paddocks and prehistoric fences of stacked rocks. The horizon stretched flat and empty. Thorley driving a rented four-wheel drive, leather interior. Tiny cardboard pine tree dangling from the rear-view mirror.

He'd asked me four times to go with them, kept saying: 'You won't have to do anything.'

'Nothing will happen.'

'You owe me one.'

There was something I liked in Thorley. A sort of killer instinct. He was the kind of guy who liked to fuck things up. You could imagine him burning things in the backyard fire as a kid, making napalm out of melting plastic. The kind of guy who might do anything at any moment.

And I wanted to be there when it happened.

Uncle and Harris join us on the road trip.

Uncle has a shaved head and is two years older than us, but seems content to idle in his immaturity. He's Thorley's connection for getting into nightclubs and obtaining warehouse quantities of prescription medications. Someone told me that they call him Uncle because one time when he was in school he had a fight with some kid, and the kid, who lived with his uncle, said he'd get his uncle to come down after school and bash him. Apparently, Uncle waited, in his light-blue school shirt, dark-blue school shorts, bag at his feet, waited for this kid and his uncle to show up. Uncle spat in the man's face and kicked him in the balls as hard as he could. The kid's uncle fell into the dust of the school car park, and Uncle, apparently, turned to this kid and said: 'Who's your uncle now?' Like movie dialogue gone horribly wrong.

As far as I can tell, Uncle is a full-time drug dealer. He is blank-faced and suspiciously quiet, seemingly calculating everything he says, drafting it a few times in his mind before speaking. Uncle has a triangle of beard below his lip and a high forehead that makes him look older. Uncle sits in the front seat, rides shotgun next to Thorley.

Harris is from our school, an energetic kid who talks too much if given the chance. He has that rich ignorance about him, the kind that can't connect with the struggles of the common world. Harrison is his whole name. Harris's family are religious, rich through building products or some such. He's effectively had everything he could ever want through his entire life systematically purchased for him in order to keep him quiet and out of the way.

Harris has longer hair, stops just above his ears, neat cut, straight lines around his sideburns and hairline. He wears a new-looking light-blue shirt and shining black shoes, looks ready to a walk straight into a nightclub, all set to go. I'm guessing it wasn't him who polished those fucking shoes.

And there we are, whispering along the coast road, watching the seawater reflect the sky out to the horizon. I remember as a kid scanning the distance for shark fins and whales leaping across the sunset. The memory smells sweet. Comforting.

Uncle speaks over his shoulder, says: 'Heard you broke some kid's fingers with a hammer at your old school.' He turns and smiles at me.

I tell him it's not as good a story as it may seem.

'Why'd they kick you out?' Uncle asks.

'I fucked up.'

And we stare at each other, Uncle waiting for more detail.

Uncle pronounces each word, says: 'What did you fuck up?'

'Uncle, shut up, man,' Thorley says from the driver's seat.

'I'm just asking him a question,' Uncle says.

'And he doesn't want to talk about it. It wasn't his fault. Some people fucked him over.'

Thorley nods to Uncle. Uncle turns back around, winds down the window. Cups his hands in front of his face to light a cigarette.

'Fuck people,' Uncle says, blows smoke out into the wind.

Where we're heading is Adelaide.

It's two o'clock when we decide to stop, walk in the sand. It's summer-day heat but the clouds have blocked the sun and the smell of rain clings to the air. Thorley tells me how they do this, take road trips to different towns. He says it's easier when no-one knows you and he takes out two pink pills, hands me one, drinks his down with a handful of seawater from the edge of the ocean. I flick mine down my throat like tablets I used to take for tonsillitis.

Thorley tells me how he's studied Royhpnol, how he can judge exactly how much a girl needs to be open to suggestion.

But first, Thorley says, we get a hotel room.

'One with a balcony,' I tell him.

The rest of the trip becomes cartoon-like in my mind, brighter colours and shapes. Uncle wraps his seatbelt around his arm to get his veins up, pushes a shining needle into his bloodstream. I watch the needle go into his skin, feel it.

'Shouldn't do that shit,' Thorley tells him.

Then I black out, staring at the dots on the roof of the car, watching the pattern raise up. It's that 3D image trick you do with your eyes, those pictures you stare at. Any image that repeats itself and you can do this. The dots raise up. I try to grab at the closer ones.

Then the car is humming, waiting for Thorley to return from the hotel reception. Thorley leads us to room thirty-six, opens the curtain to the balcony – parkland, green trees. Night is pushing the afternoon to a close.

Harris is watching one of the four in-house porn channels, some girl being fucked by men dressed as the French Foreign Legion, then it cuts out.

'$14.95 to continue,' the screen says. 'Press OK for preview.' Harris presses OK again.

Uncle is cutting his fingernails with a plastic bag over his hands, so as to not get them everywhere, then he gets his black shoes on and a shirt.

I follow his lead, get dressed for the night, pulling each sock on slowly, feeling it against the skin of my foot. I concentrate enough to ask Thorley what the fuck tablet he gave me at the beach. He tells me it was a Tic Tac, or a Warhead, or something.

'At least,' he says, 'that's what mine was.' And he smiles.

I feel like a midget walking through the city streets, the world distorted. The orange streetlights blur. My head bobs up and down as if I'm in a boat rolling over the waves. We walk past nightclub bouncers who stare, judge how many years we've been alive. I look at one big guy, imagine his fist rocking my jaw. Fat fucking fingers.

We enter the doorway, the lights bouncing off a mirror ball hanging over a tiny dance floor. The bass shaking everything. A robot voice repeating lyrics.

Uncle leans in to Thorley, who nods and slides something into Uncle's shirt pocket. Uncle sucks hard on his cigarette then disappears into the crowd, which vibrates like tiny earthquakes in time with the music. Harris is still hard from the porno channel, looks ready to fuck every girl that walks near us. Thorley just smiles, nods to the music. The strobe light flickers across his grinning face.

Thorley hands me a re-sealable plastic bag, a tiny one, says: 'Use it wisely,' and walks off through the club.

Harris is at the bar, one hand in his pocket, touches a girl on the back. She has a red singlet-top on and a tattoo at the base of her spine. Long blonde hair that tickles at her shoulders and flows down. Harris smiles at her, tilts his head back, gesturing for her to come closer. The blonde flicks her bleached hair away from him

and, as she does, Harris sees his chance to hit
her Malibu and Coke, drops a sprinkling of dust
into her glass.

My mind feels like it's coming into focus,
and I see a big guy, Maori maybe, grabbing at
Harris's shoulder. I move closer, not sure if I care
enough to help him. The guy puts a hand over
the girl's glass, stops her from taking a drink,
says something in her ear. The guy holds Harris's
shoulder, leans back to talk to his friends.

I'm close enough to hear now, hear him
saying Harris tried to drug the blonde. The big
guy's mates move up.

'Hey,' I say to the big guy. 'What the fuck did
thisss guy do?' My speech is sliding. I can taste
my heartbeat. The guy holds tight onto Harris's
shoulder, his knuckles white, making sure Harris
is going nowhere.

'Do you know him?' the big guy asks. He has
a forehead which sort of folds over the top of his
nose, his eyes just dark, black holes.

'Maybe,' I say. 'Maybe I do.'

The guy pushes me back, tells me to fuck off.
The blonde moves aside to let me stumble backwards and the lights seem so loud, flashing over
and over. Harris pushes and clutches at the big
guy's fingers clamped onto his shoulder, looks
like a monkey in a science experiment, shaking
to get free.

I gather my brain together for a second try,
the club rattling with bass sounds that move the

floorboards. There's a buzzing feeling in the roots of my teeth, and the Maori guy looks at me. And I think: *Fuck it.*

I whip a half-full glass of beer from the bar and smash it across the big kahuna's nose, shove it into his face with the heel of my hand. He lets go of Harris, puts his hands up to catch the blood he's losing. A big piece of the glass stays there, stuck through his upper lip, into his gums.

His friends stand still, shocked, as if they didn't expect so much blood to come out, spatter across the floor and the bar and their clothes. I kick as hard as I can at one of them, straight for his nuts. Some fucker grabs my head, punches me, pulls at my hair. I get enough leverage to elbow him, feel his nose click out of place. Only when I turn do I realise it's the blonde's face I've just smashed, her white-gold hair stained with specks of red.

Harris is already rushing out and I chase his lead through the crowd. Uncle comes from behind the flashing disco lights of some place, says: 'You fuckheads,' – maybe to us – then pushes people aside to get through, shoves them right into the walls. The three of us run to the four-wheel drive, Uncle pressing the unlock button on the key the whole way, rushing through the parked cars.

'Dumb cunts,' Uncle yells as we pull out of the concrete car park, the streetlights flashing by above us.

Three cars load up with guys and pull out close behind. One comes up beside us on the main street of town, and a guy in the back seat leans out the window, spits onto the four-wheel drive, yells at us through the glass. Someone inside their car hands him a club lock and Uncle runs a red light.

The guy hangs further out of the car, smashes the back passenger window with a swing of the metal steering lock, shatters glass all over the new-smelling seats and Harris, who's flinching and protecting his face.

'You fucking dickheads,' Uncle yells, maybe to us. 'Have we got anything to throw at them?'

Look around, nothing, an empty plastic bottle. Uncle accelerates through a roundabout, bounces over the gutter.

We drive away from the streetlights, out of the main town. One of the cars gives up the chase, pulls up, but the other two continue on our tail, their radiators breathing after the four-wheel drive.

We turn onto a shitty dirt road that rocks the cabin of the four-wheel drive around like a carnival ride.

'Turn the fucking lights off,' I tell Uncle, thinking the cars behind are only following our taillights through the darkness as we pull away. Without hesitating, he flicks them off. And we're drifting full-speed into the darkness.

'I guess we'll find out,' Uncle answers a question no-one asked.

The four-wheel drive bounces and squeals over the blank nothing ahead. It's like what I imagine flying a spaceship to be, without the stars flashing by. Only then do I notice Harris yelling in the back seat, screaming at the black through the windscreen, crying. He could have been doing this the whole time.

Uncle takes his hands off the wheel at one point, hovers them above it, watching, then grabs it again. Behind us, the headlights have tailed off in a different direction.

The final effects of the pink pill are scratching across the roof of my skull, calling for my heart to pump more blood, and then everything crashes forward, the gravity of the cabin changing as we jolt to a sudden stop. The top of my head cracks against the windscreen, dashboard against my chest, and I'm on the floor, traces of beach sand from people's shoes up on my cheek. The night sounds assure me I'm alive. I wonder whether Uncle and Harris are silent because they're dead. I say their names, one time each.

Then I close my eyes.

The sea breeze on my face wakes me, sunlight making me squint to see out to the sand-covered ground. Small trees and tufts of grass being pushed by the wind. The new-smelling four-wheel drive is on an angle, the front inclined downwards. The driver's door is open, letting in the light and the yakking of seagulls. Sand tinkles against the metal of the car. I can taste blood, but I have no idea where from. Somewhere, I can hear waves wash up against the earth. I push myself up and out so I can assess where I am.

The four-wheel drive has hit a ditch around fifty metres from the sea, a small embankment where the grass ends and the beach begins. The black tyres have sand all in their tread, looks like we've been driving through snow. Harris is asleep in the back, curled up between the front and back seats. Across on the beach Uncle is standing on the wet sand near the edge of the water, looking at the ground then at the horizon. His shirt collar flicking up as the ocean breathes.

'Fucking Harris,' Thorley says, standing up close to my desk in class. He puts his books up onto the table, leans over closer to my ear. 'Harris is like one of the fucking kids on *Charlie and the Chocolate Factory*, have you seen that? A moron.'

Across the room, a group of guys are laughing, talking shit to some nerd kid, the one with curly hair, the one they always push and yell at. The nerd kid ignores them as best he can.

'Don't worry,' Thorley tells me. 'That won't happen again.'

One of the guys across the room flicks a metal ruler into the back of the nerd's head. The nerd smoothes his hair down, keeps ignoring them. One of the guys, the loudest one, he looks over to us, says: 'What the fuck's going on over there? Getting a bit close aren't you, boys?'

Thorley stands up, picks up his books. Stares at the guy.

'What the fuck are you looking at?' the loud guy asks, stands up.

Thorley smiles, walks back to his desk.

Thorley runs to meet me as we leave class, kids crowded around and flowing out from the building, walking to the train station, the buses.

'You coming out tonight?' he asks.

Behind him, I notice the loud guy from class, who sees Thorley speaking to me, talks to his friends, points at us. The loud guy starts walking over, and a big guy, bleached blond, comes out of nowhere, punches the guy right in the face, drops him to the concrete.

The loud guy rolls onto his back slowly, side to side, moaning, and the big guy stands over him, fist clenched. Blood is coming from the loud guy's face and a crowd is gathering quickly. The big guy grabs his bag back from one of the other kids nearby, walks away through the crowd. The loud guy, he's not getting up, his eye closed-over and red. Looks dazed, blinking and trying to focus, his arm shaking. His face stuck in a stupid, unaware expression.

Thorley, without even looking at what's happening, he's in my face, says: 'You coming out tonight?'

M um calls, me playing PlayStation in Thorley's apartment, and Uncle says: 'What the fuck is that ring-tone?' He has no shirt on, sitting on the couch and waiting for his turn beside me, staring at the TV screen. Outside is sunlight, peeking through the gaps in the blinds, which are swaying slightly from me jumping and moving in time with the game. I put the phone to my ear, pause the game.

'Do you still live at our house?' Mum says. 'We were thinking of putting your room up for rent.'

'Yes, Mum.' And when I say 'Mum' I make sure I put extra emphasis on it, loud enough for Uncle to hear so he knows not to say anything. I hand him the controller, peel myself off the couch and walk to the balcony. Squint into the sudden brightness outside, shut the door behind me.

'So, what have you been up to?' Mum asks.

Since Dad started bringing in bigger money Mum hasn't had to work, spends her days

42

cleaning the house and talking to the dog and watching soap operas. She avoids spending too much money, still not used to having disposable income. Mum, sometimes she'll say things and you know she's been thinking over how to word them for a long time. She's acted out this conversation before, imagined my responses.

'Sorry, I've just been out a bit this week.'

'Out? What about school? They called your father, you know.'

My mind flicks to panic mode, maybe they've investigated Mrs Arthur, maybe she's remembered everything.

'What for?'

'They said you missed a couple of classes,' Mum says, and I relax, my sweat pores closing up again. 'They call when you miss a class at this school.'

'That was a train problem, Mum, delayed service.'

'Well, where have you been for the last week?'

'I haven't been away *all* week. I've got a friend who lives in the city, closer to the school, so I've been staying at his house a bit, don't have to get up so early.'

'Is that okay with his parents?'

'Yeah, he lives with his uncle.' And I look in to see Uncle, topless, standing and yelling at the PlayStation screen. He has a black tattoo on his shoulder blade but I can't make out the detail.

'Maybe I should give his uncle a call and speak to him,' Mum says. She'll be thinking this one over for weeks.

'You can if you want – I have the number in my phone, so I'll text it to you later.'

'How is the new school going?'

Rich kids, spoilt all their lives, fucking whingeing, bitching, crying and buying drugs and cars and getting fucked up.

'It's fine,' I tell Mum.

'So you're making friends then?'

'It's. Fine. Mum.'

'Okay. Can you please be home for dinner tonight?'

'Um, I'll . . .' Try to recall our plan for tonight. Try to forget what happened last night. Image of a naked brunette being fucked against the nightclub toilet wall, a hand on her neck.

'It's your father's birthday.'

And I never remember these fucking things. 'Will Dad be there?'

'He told me he would make sure everything is taken care of so he can have a night off. He's been busy, stressing about some new deal.'

'He's always busy, Mum.'

'He's doing very well. Will you be home?'

Inside, Uncle throws the PlayStation controller, bounces it off the TV screen, goes to the fridge to get a beer. Thorley comes out of his room, talks to Uncle, up close. Soon, Uncle will be going on a drug run.

'Will you be home? Please?' Mum says in my ear.

'Yeah, Mum,' I tell her. 'I'll be there.'

Train ride, always rocks me to sleep. Watch the houses and graffiti-covered fences flash by, my eyes scanning back and forth to focus as we pass. Sometimes I watch people doing this same thing, their pupils darting from side to side like they have a brain problem.

A group of schoolgirls get into the carriage, white socks to their knees and bags hanging from their elbows. They talk too loud about TV shows and bullshit, become my fucking unrequested celebrity gossip update. One of them is pretty, good tits, her shirt buttons undone enough to see the edge of her bra. The others are just okay.

And I realise I have just picked my target, without even meaning it. I have decided who I would take home. This is what Thorley does. Imagine the pretty girl naked and unconscious on Thorley's carpet. My fingers grabbing at her skin. Clench my teeth, turn my head away. Stare out at the passing houses, roads, rail bridge, parked cars, billboard. Ignore the sudden violence in my head.

Mum comes to the door when I arrive, gives me a hug. I can't remember her ever doing this before.

'Where have you been?' she asks.

'Nowhere. What's for dinner?'

'Beef stroganoff.'

'Is that what Dad wanted for his birthday dinner?'

'I couldn't get on to him today, but I know he likes it.' Mum smiles, stands in front of me for a moment, then returns to the kitchen. New blinds up over the windows.

I walk through to my room, single bed, posters of comic book heroes and rap bands and video game characters. Stickers from when I was a kid still stuck to the cupboard door. Mum's cleaned it up, everything neat and folded. Plug my phone into the charger and drop my wallet on the desk.

Mum's watching *Wheel of Fortune* while she dances through the house, smells of cooking meat and cleaning products at the same time.

'Where's Dad at?' I yell to her.

'He's on his way home, should be here in five minutes.'

'Is he pissed off at me for the school thing?'

'I don't think so. He didn't mention it.'

And I go outside to say hi to the dog, push his big head around and scratch behind his ears.

'How you been, boy?' I say, his tail wagging.

Dad comes home, slams the door behind himself, carrying his jacket and laptop computer bag. He sees me on the couch but says nothing, moves to the next room. Mum rushes dinner out and

46

we sit down, Dad mixing his food together with his utensils, and when Mum asks him about work he says: 'Please don't, I just don't want to think about work for ten minutes.'

'Stroganoff okay?' Mum asks.

'It's good, thank you,' Dad tells her, then to me: 'Your teacher called, said you missed a class.'

Mum responds for me, says: 'It was a train delay. They have so many train delays and cancellations these days.' And her tone is like *Why is that?*

'Can you put in a little more effort in future?' Dad asks, his head facing down to his food, eating faster than me. His thinning hair is revealing more of his shiny scalp these days. I nod back to him, mouthful of beef.

'He's doing well, got some new friends, haven't you, son?' Mum smiles to me.

Right now, Uncle and Thorley are out on the streets, a drug run, then they'll be out in the city, the clubs. The lights across the faces of the girls as they dance in the darkness, moving their hips. Their tits. Thorley and Uncle watching, picking their targets. Taking them back to the apartment. Getting them naked. I've got to get out of here.

'More effort?' I say, and Mum looks at me, serious expression, shakes her head from side to side. She knows the tone I'm using here. 'What could I do?'

47

Dad looks up from his dinner. 'We are paying a lot of money to send you to that school,' he says.

'He's fine, he's doing good.' Mum puts a hand onto Dad's shoulder as she speaks.

Dad points his food-covered fork in my direction, says: 'So don't mess this up.'

'Fuck off,' I tell him, and Mum is shaking her head. 'You don't believe me about the train?'

'I'm not saying I don't – ' Dad starts.

'Yes, you are saying that, Dad. You don't believe me. I made a couple of mistakes but I'm doing okay at this school, but you can't let it go, can you?'

Dad stares at me, unsure what to say. Mum is still shaking her head, her eyes begging me to stop.

I stand up, kick my chair back against the wall, say: 'Do you wonder why I stay away from here, Mum?' And I go to my room, get my phone, my wallet, jacket, and Mum stands in my doorway.

'Are you going out?' she asks, but I don't answer. 'Your Dad's stressed at the moment, can't we just calm down and . . .'

But my mind is already in the city and I walk past her, towards the hallway, Dad sitting alone at the dinner table as I go by, elbows up on the table, hands together. And Mum catches up, stands in front of me, smiling uncomfortably. Looks unsure how to start what she wants to say.

'Please don't go,' she says.

Stare her down, silent.

She looks away from me for a moment, moves her lips without speaking. Looks back at my eyes. 'I love you. Okay?' Mum says, puts a hand up and nods, once, as if to say 'that's all', then walks away, back down the hallway. Runs her fingers through her long hair, rests them on the back of her neck.

Call Thorley's number as I walk towards the train station.

'How would your mother feel about what you've done?' Dr Jessica Snowden asks, watching for my reaction.

Dr Jessica Snowden is the psychologist. 'Call me Jess,' she says. After everything fucked up, they assigned Dr Jess to fix me. Part of my punishment.

Dr Jessica Snowden is a psychologist, not a psychiatrist. See, the difference is psychiatrists are medical doctors first, who then go on to specialise in psychiatry. Psychologists are not. This means only psychiatrists can prescribe medication, drugs. Dr Jessica Snowden cannot prescribe medication. What I know about Dr Jess is she likes horse-riding.

'That's how I relax,' she says. 'How do you relax?'

With Dr Jessica Snowden everything is a question. She watches every move I make, monitors it, takes notes. Everything means something. Reaching for my throat, smoothing my hair. Each action is another shorthand message scribbled onto her notepad.

This is how they connect the dots.

This is how they fix you.

Dr Jessica Snowden is tall and wears skirts that stop just above her knees. She's maybe in her early thirties, wears glasses and dark shades of lipstick. Dr Jessica Snowden ties her blonde hair back most days, and when she does she looks like an extra from a Robert Palmer video clip. She's not beautiful, but she's not unattractive.

What else I know about Dr Jessica Snowden is she is very neat, she hates things out of place. She likes cats, has two at home. Dr Jessica Snowden grew up in a suburban house with one sister, her father a firefighter, her mother a nurse, and when she tells me this I say my parents are not to blame for who I am. I tell her not to bother going down that path. They have nothing to do with anything.

They did their best.

We meet on Mondays and Thursdays. This breaks up the week. We meet in her office, a white, clinical-looking place with hard-spined magazines in the waiting room. Her secretary has a piece of paper attached to her filing cabinet that says 'I am Attraction in Action'. The secretary is neither of these things. Lying to yourself can play a big part in mental health.

Dr Jessica Snowden talks to me about music she likes, movies she's seen, all conversation points so we can get to know each other, become friends. Maybe if she gets the right question I'll open up to her. Spill my guts. Tell her every secret of my life. Then maybe she can connect the dots, fix me up. Tell me I'm not alone in suffering 'Insert name here' Syndrome, pat me on the shoulder as I cry. I know how it works. Years of school counsellors and people who just want to help.

When I look at Dr Jessica Snowden I wonder what she is thinking. I think of the things psychopaths might have told her. I think of what stories she could tell of crazed deviants and desperate housewives.

Because she deals with a lot of young offenders, on her desk she has a Simpsons doll. Bart. Something to show she's into the same things you are. Something in common.

'I like action films,' she says. '*Braveheart*, that's one of my favourites. But I also – and I know it's a bit corny – but I like romance films too.' Dr Jess sees she's getting nowhere with the film conversation, adjusts her seating position, decides to change tack.

And Dr Jessica Snowden asks how my mother would feel.

This is how it goes with Dr Jess: a soft question, then a hard one. Pat me nicely, then punch me in the face, real quick, see how I react. I smile at her.

'No idea,' I tell her. 'Maybe you should ask her.'
'Maybe I will.'

'Yeah, I'm sure she'd love to have a chat with you.'

Dr Jessica Snowden puts her head down, writes something. 'I've spoken to her before,' she says.

And it feels like the air is being squeezed out of me, a burning pain through my chest, as if my muscles are turning to concrete, rising to my neck. Fucking hurts. I want to ask Dr Jess how Mum looks, how she's doing. What did Mum say about me? But fuck that. That's what Dr Jessica Snowden wants.

She lifts her head back up, stares at me. Rests her hands in her lap.

Fuck her.

'So why are you asking me then?' I say.

'I want to know how you feel, what you think.'

'I told you my parents have nothing to do with this.'

Dr Jessica Snowden nods, writes notes, her pen scratching across the notepad. The noise makes me squeeze hard onto the metal frame of my chair.

Makes me want to stab that fucking pen into her face.

'They get edgy, so don't fuck around,' Uncle says as I walk with him along the city footpath.

It's night-time, so the streets are crowded with people in their newest clothes, drunk and yelling for taxis and looking at reflections of themselves in the shop windows. We walk past a bar, a movie theatre, people running across the street, cars pressing their horns.

What happened is Thorley told me that Uncle had borrowed his car, taken it into the city. Thorley told me to meet up with him, get a ride back to the apartment.

'We're going over there.' And Uncle points to a video game arcade, flashing green and red lights. Kids spilling out onto the footpath in front of the place. Guys with bleached streaks in their black hair, a guy with a tattoo on his neck. Spider web, how original.

Uncle leads me through, shakes hands and touches fists with people as we go, leads me upstairs to a pool hall, a dark room with smoke drifting through the light above the green tables. Everyone stops and looks when we come in. Big dark-skinned guys with shaved heads. Skinny pale-faced kids with pimples. An older guy in a 50 Cent T-shirt, his long hair starting to turn grey.

Uncle leads me through to the back of the room, shakes hands with a guy who's sitting on a bar stool next to a pool table, a couple of other guys lingering close by, watching. The guy on the stool is Asian, straight black hair swept away from his face. Skinny arms poking out of his red short-sleeve shirt. Big silver bracelet around his wrist. This guy is not playing pool.

Uncle says something to him and the guy shows no emotion or expression, just looks at Uncle's face. Then Uncle leads the way back out of the pool hall, down past the video games, kids jumping on the flashing arrows of the dancing machines, back out onto the street. A wave of wind sweeping across the concrete.

'Now we wait,' Uncle tells me.

'Wait for what?'

Uncle stops walking about a block away from the arcade, looks up and then down the footpath. 'Where the fuck are you from?' he asks.

'Out in the suburbs, why?'

But Uncle has already forgotten the question, lighting a cigarette, leaning up on the darkened window of a clothing store, locked up and closed.

'Adelaide, that was pretty fucked up, huh?' Uncle opens his eyes wide when he speaks, raises his eyebrows as he ends the question.

'Has anything like that happened before?'

'One time we were at a fucking Irish pub and there was this bridal party group, a chick on her hen's night, and Thorley decided he wanted to take home the bride-to-be. She's wearing a crown and shit.' Uncle waves his cigarette like a halo around his head. 'Thorley hits her drink and starts dragging her away from the group, and they keep pulling her back and they look all worried. One of them calls the fucking fiancé, gets him to come and save her. Big, bald dude. He was fucking pissed off.' Uncle shakes his head.

'What happened?' I ask him.

'Troy fucked him up, grabbed the dude by the shoulders and rammed his spine against the corner of the bar. Rammed him against it over and over. I think Thorley kicked him in the face too.' Uncle laughs. 'Imagine the fucking wedding photos.' Takes another drag on his cigarette, shifts his eyes to me.

'Who's Troy?' I ask. Uncle looks surprised.

'You haven't met Troy yet? You will.' Blows smoke out into the night. 'How'd you end up hanging out with Thorley?'

'He helped me with something at school.'

'Mrs Arthur, huh?' Uncle smiles.

'How'd *you* end up hanging out with Thorley?' I ask.

'He calls me when he needs shit,' Uncle says, looks back down the street, smoke flowing out of his mouth. 'He helped me out one time.'

Uncle leans forward to look out past me up the footpath. Headlights and noise coming our way from both directions. 'Fuck this, let's go do something,' he says, leads the way up the street.

We walk into an adult cinema, Uncle staring at me and smiling as he walks through the door. A big guy nods to us as we pass him, dressed in all black, number 53 on a card pinned to his chest. Uncle pats the guy on the back.

We walk into the cinema, sit up the back because the show has already started. Old guys wanking, their bodies shaking as they watch. One big fat guy with curly hair sitting in the middle section. Barely able to fit into one seat. Stale smell all through the place.

On the screen, some little Indian girl, long straight black hair, she's being fucked up the ass by a big guy, hairy chest, gritting his teeth as he forces his cock into her. Cheesy soundtrack, as if they are trying to fit the cliché. The big guy is hammering hard, really giving it to the little girl, her white teeth contrasted against her dark skin. Looks like it's hurting her more than she expected. Close-up on the guy's penis penetrating her anus. In and out. Over and over.

Uncle watches intently, concentrating.

'We're gonna go get some tonight,' he tells me, adjusts his seating position, leans back.

Uncle nods as he stares towards the screen, the flashing images lighting up his features. Movie dialogue echoing through the speakers. 'You fucking love that,' the big guy tells the Indian girl.

We walk back out to the street, and over on the other side a group of young girls are lined up to get into some shitty venue, all high heels and short skirts. Door bitch wears a white cowboy hat and a black fur coat, looks pissed off at everything. She grits her teeth when she takes a drag on her cigarette.

'Which one would you do?' Uncle asks, surveying the line of girls, all perfectly placed hair and too much make-up.

'I'd go the redhead in that group.' I say, pointing but trying not to be obvious about it.

'Yeah, redhead chicks are fucking hot,' Uncle nods, without looking at me. 'She's good. She'd have a good pussy too. We'll come back here.'

And he leads me back along the street, into Chinatown, to a multi-level car park, up to the fourth level. Uncle approaches a group of guys standing by a car, look like they're about to leave. Uncle nods to them as he gets closer, and one of the guys opens the back door, brings out a plastic shopping bag, the handles tied in a knot, hands the bag to Uncle. Uncle presses money into the guy's hand and we leave, back across the noise of the city, back to Thorley's car.

We drive to Thorley's apartment, Uncle handing the bag to Thorley as we come in. Troy is there too, sitting in front of the TV, his big fucking body squashed into the couch. I recognise his blond hair straight away. The big guy. Troy doesn't play sport but he does weights and eats steroid tablets from Thorley. He's tall, my fist can fit into the ridges of his He-Man pecs. He bleaches his hair to white and smiles with crooked teeth.

'Hey, guys,' he waves. 'Good to see you.'

Thorley throws a shining, wrapped package of something over to Troy's smiling face, then examines the other packages one by one, drops them on the bench. Thorley counts them, points at each without making a sound. Drums his hands onto the bench in front of him.

'We going out?' Thorley asks.

Uncle, standing behind me, he pats me on the back.

'He's picked a ginger tonight,' Uncle says.

Thorley smiles at me, puts a pill of some kind onto his tongue, bends over to drink water straight from the tap.

'A ginger?' Troy says, standing up and stretching his massive arms.

Thorley shakes his head, wipes at his face. 'Let's go get her,' he says.

The key to sleight of hand is to always be natural. Thorley explained this to me, told me about how sleight of hand tricks worked. Thorley had done an amateur magic class, signed a 'Magician's Oath' certificate and everything, all stars and wands and top hats around the border of the writing. He'd read books and researched how this worked, the psychology of the great magicians. This is how Thorley operates, a perfectionist.

'Dai Vernon,' Thorley tells me, 'was the best sleight of hand magician of all time.'

Switches, changes, double lifts. Magicians will do all they can to make sure no-one knows how these fucking tricks work. The key is misdirection. The key, Thorley tells me, is timing.

This is what we used out in clubs, lurking around bars and tables, waiting for the right time to move on a target. Normally, a second person also assists, stands guard to make sure the sleight of hand works, makes sure no-one is paying too much attention.

'That's the trick,' Thorley says. 'What you want is attention, but not too much attention.' Thorley speaks in stern directions, uses hand motions to emphasise his critical points. 'Magicians can get away with this in front of crowds of thousands. Our stage is dimly lit, has no central focus and the majority of the crowd is drunk. Our gigs are fucking easy.'

Bumping into someone is the most basic method, getting up close and infecting their drink. The idea of misdirection is that a larger action will cover a smaller one. Though the technicalities of bumping into someone are not so precise, they are effective and will get the job done in most cases.

Reach across the table to brush something off the shoulder of the target. Go to take drinks from the bar that aren't yours 'by accident'. Separate the target from their drink for just a moment when they rest it down. These are the basics. Larger action hiding smaller.

Thorley could do this right in front of their faces. Right up in front of the bartender, the security guard. Thorley was smooth, an expert at timing and precision. He'd spent months working on perfecting his skills, becoming as good as a real magician. He'd push himself too, tell us what he was about to do before trying it.

'That girl there. Count backwards from ten,' he'd tell us.

The first couple of times you do this are

61

fucking hard. The fear of being caught floods through you, like when you're shoplifting or stealing money from your mum's purse, second-guessing yourself at every step. You notice everyone who looks at you, everyone who passes, the busboy collecting empty glasses, the bouncer. You try to keep an eye on them to make sure they're not watching. In your head you have to keep telling yourself to be natural.

Be natural.

Be natural.

Squeeze your thumb along the bag to get the powder out.

Keep walking.

After a couple of times it's almost too easy. Take me to a magic show and I'll ruin it for you, point out every misdirect he's using. Seven of hearts, my fucking ass.

Step on a toe, pretend you've hurt your hand. Thorley would even yell in a target's face, straight out of nowhere, get up real close. Bigger action covering smaller.

'Remember, you are in control here.'

'These little girls, they know nothing.'

'Be natural.'

This is how Thorley explained it to all of us. And we were fucking good at it.

Thorley has a girl leaning onto him, falling onto him, drags her into the apartment. The girl has white-blonde hair and clear lip-gloss, and her eyes are rolling back but she's pretty, tight jeans and a singlet-top. She's not speaking, barely aware of what's happening.

Thorley pushes through the doorway, knocks her shoulder against the frame as he goes, pulls her over to the couch, drops her body. She slides off the edge of the cushions, hits the carpet hard. Thorley goes to pick her up, hesitates, then leaves her, her hair spread across and away from her head on the floor. She's breathing fast.

Harris stumbles in behind us and six beers in, Harris is making no sense, erratic. He is laughing at nothing and bumping into everything.

'Shit,' Harris says, staring at the blonde girl. 'I saw her, man, she is so fucking hot.'

Thorley shuts the front door and moves into the next room, undoing his shirt as he goes.

Harris leans up onto my shoulder, me on the couch, looking over the blonde.

'She's so fucking hot,' he tells me. 'Look at those tits.'

And Harris leans over, reaches out to feel them, like a blind man without his cane. I don't say anything, just sit in my chair and watch him. Harris grabs her breast, squeezes it hard then lets go, spreads his fingers. He looks back over his shoulder at me, looks like a kid sneaking a peak at his Christmas presents.

Harris turns back to the blonde, lifts her singlet-top up, her perfect tanned skin. The blonde moves slightly, still breathing hard and her eyes rolling back, flittering. Harris lifts her top up further, reveals her red bra. She has perfect tits, firm, tanned. She must sunbake topless. Harris puts his hands one on each tit, feels them, makes a satisfied noise under his breath. He's fucking loving this.

The blonde rolls her head to the side, her eyes closed but still moving beneath her eyelids. Harris rips her bra away from her nipples, which are big, pink. He pushes his fingers across her skin, folds her nipple over. Harris leans down, sucks on her tit, makes a slurp sound. And Thorley comes back into the room, wearing nothing but a pair of shorts.

'What the fuck?' Thorley yells, and Harris jumps, pulls at her clothes, tries to cover her up.

'Shit, man.' Harris looks frightened, puts his

hands up in the air. 'Fuck, I'm sorry, man.' Harris moves back from the blonde, her shirt all a mess and the bottom of her red bra up across her tit, pushing into her skin.

'You fucking cockhead, what the fuck are you doing?' Thorley yells again.

'I'm sorry, man, I saw her there too, you know, she's just so fucking – '

'Now you have to fuck her,' Thorley tells him, standing over us both.

'What? No, she's yours, man, it's cool.'

'Get your pants off and fuck her. Right there.'

'No, no, look – ' And Harris stands up.

'You get back down there and you fuck her, right now.' Thorley points to the blonde. 'Right there.'

Harris shakes his head and Thorley screams at him: 'Fucking do it.'

Harris struggles to get her top off over her head, gets it tangled in her arms which are just hanging, useless. He drags her tight jeans down her legs, takes her shoes off, pulls her underwear down – fully shaven pussy, tiny flecks of stubble across it. The blonde opens and closes her mouth, breathes deep and slow, her arms all out to the side after Harris's undressing, her hair's a mess. Looks like an abandoned Barbie doll.

Harris takes his pants off, the loose change in his pocket falling out as he drops them to the floor and he scrambles to the carpet to pick up the coins but Thorley kicks at his hands, stops him.

Harris pulls his T-shirt off and Thorley walks over to the kitchen, gets two Coronas from the fridge, presses one against my chest. Harris is skinny and pale and has pimples on his body. He holds one hand over his cock as he pushes his underwear down to his feet. He looks up at Thorley, his eyes pleading.

'Now fuck her,' Thorley demands.

Harris kneels down beside the blonde, pushes her legs apart. Puts his fingers inside her.

'What the fuck are you doing?' Thorley yells again.

Harris shakes when he hears it, pulls his fingers away in panic. 'She won't be wet, I – '

'Here.' And Thorley steps over, pours his beer onto her bald pussy. 'Now she's fucking wet.'

Harris kneels between her legs, gets his penis up close, aims it towards her, has trouble getting inside her, clumsily pushing and having his dick slide back up to the top of her pussy.

'What the fuck?' Thorley yells at him.

'Sorry, sorry,' Harris whimpers. He forces his cock into her, thrusts, stabs his hips forward in tiny movements, pushing deeper between her thighs.

'Grab her tit,' Thorley says, and Harris quickly reaches forward, grabs it like someone would hold a door knob. He looks back over his shoulder at us, then turns to face forward again, looks panicked.

Harris starts fucking faster, harder, starts squeezing his fingers over her tit. His hips slapping onto her skin. He makes noises at the start of each breath. His hand closes tighter on her breast and her skin is red, strained from his grip. Harris moves both hands to her hips, lifts her to push his cock in further, starts hissing each time he inhales.

Thorley jumps up from the couch, belts his half-full bottle of Corona against the side of Harris's head. The bottle makes a sharp, high pitch howl as it rebounds off his skull, doesn't break. Harris turns quickly, one hand rubbing where the bottle has hit him, the other hand up in front of him ready to fend Thorley off. His cock flaps against his legs, shining and wet from the beer and her pussy. The girl makes a noise, like snoring but not as deep.

Harris is flinching, one arm trembling in front of him, speaks quickly: 'Fuck, fuck, I'm sorry.'

Thorley brings the bottle back around, gets ready to hit Harris again, holds it up above his shoulder.

'If you ever fuck with me like this again . . .' Thorley spits the words at Harris's face, right up close, and Harris, he's crying, his mouth open as if ready to scream. Thorley flicks the bottle at Harris chest, what's left of the beer spilling onto his naked legs.

'You get rid of this,' Thorley says. He stands,

towering over Harris. Thorley looks down on the blonde, shoves her naked leg with his foot. 'Get this shit out of my house.'

Thorley walks into the next room, the door closing behind him. Harris, naked, tears across his face, slumped on the carpet, he rubs at his head, looks up at me.

'What should I do?' he cries.

And I walk out to the balcony, close the sliding door behind me.

TV wakes me up, Thorley flicking channels and sitting on the floor in front of the couch where I'm sleeping. He changes through them quickly, staring at the screen.

'What did Harris do with the girl?' Thorley asks without looking away from the flashing images.

'I don't know, I went outside, left him to it.'

Thorley nods, the channels switching quickly, lighting up the room. 'We've got to be careful of these fucking guys,' Thorley tells me. 'They're gonna fuck it up for all of us.'

Thorley stops flicking channels, some infomercial for an abdominal workout machine, a woman folding the thing down and sliding it under her bed.

'I need you, man.' he says. 'You're not a fuckhead like them.'

TV flashes to some musclebound guy, smiling as he crunches his stomach, showing off all his white teeth.

'You hear me?'

69

'Yeah,' I answer. 'Has that happened before?'

Thorley shakes his head.

'And it won't happen again,' he says. Thorley presses the off button, the screen fizzing into darkness. 'Harris is an idiot, he's always a risk.'

'Why hang around with him then?'

'Sometimes it's good to have his extra cash handy. His dad's wallet is never too far away,' Thorley says. 'I've given him everything.'

Thorley sits for a moment, still.

'We'll get him back for that,' Thorley tells me, walks back through the shadows, his bedroom door closing behind him.

I met Aleesa at one of Thorley's parties, me leaning against a door frame watching the crowd move through his white and brown shaded lounge room. Watching the same people having the same conversations they had last week, drinking enough to forget the details so they can restate their clever points, yelling at each other over the music. Bass-beat electro noise filling the room.

A group of three girls look ignorant of everyone around them, dance together on the carpet in front of the widescreen TV, running their hands all over each other and rolling their hips. Sometimes they break and storm the bathroom together, and when they come out they sniff and touch at their noses, try to make it look like part of their dance routine.

Aleesa sees me, stares at me for a moment, then walks over, stands in front of me with her head tilted to the side. She has long dark hair, dead straight with white-blonde stretches. She's wearing a black strapless dress that shows off her dark tanned skin. Aleesa puts her head down to sip her drink, rolls her dark eyes back up to me, smiling.

'I heard you fucked a teacher at your school,' she says.

'Not entirely true.'

'The science teacher, right? That woman's gonna get an addiction to that shit Thorley gives her.'

'What do you mean?' I ask her.

Aleesa smiles. 'Who's your pick tonight?' she says, turns to face the girls dancing on the carpet.

'You're looking pretty good,' I tell her. She shifts her eyes slowly back to me, the straw from her drink gently held between her teeth. She holds her glass up to my face.

'You gonna drug me?'

'I don't do that.'

'Ha. Bullshit. All you guys do it'

'So why are you here then? Aren't you worried?'

'I can take care of myself.'

A young guy joins the dancers, rubbing his hands across the clothes of the girls. Aleesa catches my eyes watching them.

'Some girls don't really care,' she says, and walks off into the crowd, looking back over her shoulder. Her dark eyes staring from beneath the edges of her fringe.

On the couch is Susannah Lockshardt, gathering all of the attention in the room. She is not immediately beautiful. What she is is famous. And here she is, reclining on Thorley's white leather, talking shit to some random red-haired girl who is smiling and fake-laughing through the conversation. Every few minutes, the redhead looks around the room, checks who's noticed that she is speaking to Susannah Lockshardt. She and Susannah are having a conversation.

It's a strange feeling seeing fame up close. It is painfully human in its celebrity, without the gloss wrap over it. No change-channel protection. Any skin problems, any close-up difference to the image is amplified. The blending of media fiction and reality put the world before you into a plastic state. Life feels like a TV show, a modelling shoot. Cameras ready. Smile.

Susannah Lockshardt is not as overpowering as I thought she would be, her size a miniature version of my mental image. She has been doing TV commercials for what seems like years, advertising jeans, bent over and looking back, shaking her diet-motivating ass. Advertising make-up with her polyester skin. The latest cola on her lips. The latest faded, barely there, sugar-free whatever. She smiles across freeways from billboards, like an angel framed against the sky. She winks from the back of taxi cabs and the sides of buses, her image imbedded into memory.

And here she is. Her hair looking average-girl

tousled, her too-white teeth glowing like neon against her tanned, almost orange skin. Thorley told me how Uncle used to work at a nightclub and Uncle used to see Susannah Lockshardt there all the time, says she left with a different guy each week. Uncle, he also told Thorley how she hates condoms, refuses to let a guy use one. 'She's a dirty bitch,' Thorley says.

Thorley serves her a colourful cocktail, smiling and starting conversation, says: 'Welcome to my party.' She seems to flirt out of instinct. Susannah 'Licks Hard', she moves her tongue across her gloss-shine lips as she finishes each sip. She tells us about celebrities who've bent her over balconies of the finest hotels. Football stars who've come too soon. TV actors who call when their wives are out of town.

Susannah touches her tits when she talks about having girls go down on her. Her eyes blink slowly, and she talks about fucking three guys at one time, how they cheered each other on. Susannah drinks down the last bubbles of inhibition from her glass, drops it bouncing across the cream.

Thorley says something in her ear, over the hammering bass sounds that fill the room. Susannah grabs hold of his shirt, says: 'Fuck, yes,' and kisses him hard.

Across the room, Aleesa is watching me, smiling. She points into her glass, then at Susannah Lockshardt.

Susannah falls onto the bed in her underwear, fumbling to get her bra from her body. She's saying: 'Yes, yes,' impatiently. Thorley tells me he's given her enough to knock the normal person out cold. Susannah grabs at the air, her naked body with triangles of untanned sections over her nipples. Her pubic hair neatly cropped in a thin strip. Troy comes in with a video camera, closes the door to the voices and music outside.

'Fu-uck,' Troy laughs excitedly.

Susannah writhes on her back, unaware of his presence. Thorley takes off his shirt, drops his pants to the carpet. He leans over Susannah Lockshardt on his hands and knees, examines her body. Troy fumbles with the buttons of the camera, his hard-on pushing at his jeans. Thorley licks at her tits, Susannah is mumbling, 'Yes . . .'

'Yes.'

Thorley puts his mouth over her right breast, grabs the other, hard. Susannah tilts her head back, lets out a noise. Thorley slides his hand down between her legs, pushes his fingers inside her. Troy swings around for a better angle of the action.

'Now fuck her,' Troy laughs, barely able to hold himself back. Susannah reaches for Thorley's underwear, struggles to get her hand on his dick. One of her eyes is half-open. Troy hands me the camera, takes his T-shirt off over his head.

'Fuck this,' Troy says, taking down his pants. Troy slaps Thorley's hand away from her pussy, pushes his cock into her, and she beats the bed with her hand. 'Are you getting this?' Troy asks.

Thorley takes off his underwear, puts his penis into her mouth. Susannah seems unclear on what's happening, her mouth wide open around it. Thorley grabs her hair, rough, guides her head. Troy hammers at her, his naked ass quivering as their hips make contact. Thorley starts jerking himself off near Susannah's face. I'm thinking of how this might make a good advertisement.

Try our new Miracoil bed springs.

Men can't resist the new fragrance from Ralph Lauren.

I'm thinking: *That wink on the side of the bus will never be the same. That angel among the clouds on the freeway.*

The room smells of sweat as Thorley and Troy perform for the camera. Through the lens I pretend this isn't real. This is fiction. Plastic.

Someone opens the door, some girl peeking in, and Thorley yells: 'Lock the fucking door.'

And I kick it closed, flick the lock.

A sound echoes from Susannah's throat, her body convulses upward. She vomits blue liquid up onto the sheets, burping and coughing it out, dribbling down her chin. That sharp smell of alcohol rushes through to the back of my throat. Thorley shoves her face away with his left hand, keeps masturbating with his right. He comes across her cheek and neck. Semen and vomit and smeared make-up.

Thorley wipes his hand down Susannah's chest, leaves a shining trail between her tits. He sniffs at his fingers, looks disgusted. She's not moving, her head tilted away.

And Troy, hammering at Susannah Locks-hardt, looks into the camera. Smiles. Puts one thumb in the air. And he says: 'You gonna fuck her?'

It's later, when the party is dying down, that Aleesa sneaks up behind me, touches my shoulder.

'How was she?' she asks.

'Ask Thorley,' I tell her.

Aleesa smiles. 'Were you too scared to do it in front of the other boys?' she pouts.

'She's not my type.'

Aleesa takes my hand, holds it up over her shoulder as she leads me away. Dumps her drink as we pass the kitchen bench, leads me out the front door. In the elevator, she presses the button for the ground floor, rushes her head over to kiss me, presses me against the wall. Taste her lips, her tongue. She smiles at me as the doors open, leads the way out, still holding my hand.

Aleesa pulls me along the footpath in the night, the rows of headlights flashing by us. She drags me through the parked cars and onto the green grass of the park, a miniature reminder of nature in the middle of the buildings that cry across the night. She pulls me to the darkness of a tree, shadowed by the streetlights across the way, leans her back up onto the bark, her dark eyes staring at me.

'What do you want to do with me?' she asks.

'Nothing.'

'Nothing? You mean I'm not good enough for you?' Aleesa feigns offence.

I slide my hand up her leg, beneath her dress, feel the lace edges of her underwear.

'What did you mean before?' I ask her, my mouth close to her neck. 'When you said that some girls don't really care.'

'Everyone knows you boys. Everyone knows what you guys do.' Aleesa grips the hair on the back of my head. 'Some just don't care. Some like the drama of it. Some take it as a compliment, in a weird kind of way,' Aleesa laughs.

'But not you?'

'I can take care of myself.'

I slide my hand down into her underwear, work my fingers inside her. Aleesa sighs.

'Fucken kids,' she says. Aleesa puts her hand down to mine, pushes my fingers to her clitoris, gently guides me. She takes her hand away, lets me continue. Aleesa jerks slightly against the tree, closes her eyes, breathes harder. Behind us, a couple walk by along the path, holding hands.

I watch the wind blow Aleesa's hair across her face under the orange glow of the streetlight, her head tilted back, eyes closed. The distant sounds of the city. A car horn. A scream.

Aleesa pushes me back with both hands, turns around, points her ass towards me, hands up on the tree. I lift her dress to her waist, flip it up so I can see her red g-string, pull it down to her knees, unzip my pants. I pull her hips into mine, her naked skin cold in the night air.

'Harder,' Aleesa tells me, and I push myself into her, her ass on my hip bones. 'Harder', she says and I come too quickly, letting out exhausted gasps. Aleesa moans in time with me. I pull my pants up, fall back onto the grass.

Aleesa lies down next to me, her body crushing the dead leaves. A billboard of Susannah Lockshardt is peeking through the trees that line the border of the park. She's advertising make-up. I roll over, pretend I can't feel her eyes staring me down. And Aleesa's there, looking at me, smiling. She reaches her hand out to touch my face. I look up to the gap of stars through the branches and leaves above us.

'Try to spot a satellite,' Aleesa whispers, her lips tingling my ear. 'They're like stars, but moving.'

Aleesa, she really doesn't care who I am, where we are. She never even asked me my name.

Aleesa kisses my forehead, stands up, straightens her dress, her shadow looming across everything. The leaves blow around her as if they are in her command. As if she made the wind blow at just that moment. Beautiful. She smiles, laughs, sort of, then she's gone. I watch her waving her hand at the road, a taxi slowing by her.

'Did you have trouble finding girlfriends?' Dr Jessica Snowden asks, me leaning back as far as I can on my chair, staring at the roof of her office. I try to make sure I don't change position. Point your feet, turn your body; Dr Jess is watching for these things. Keeping your lips together could mean you're concerned.

'Nah. No problem,' I answer, smile with my mouth open. Mouth wide open could mean you're too happy.

'What about Aleesa Desca?' Dr Jessica Snowden asks, her pen already touching the paper, waiting. 'What happened with her?'

I laugh, just one single 'huh' with my mouth closed. Try to keep calm. Ears going red means you're angry. Flashback to voices yelling through the crack in Thorley's door. Uncle's fingers bent back too far. The policeman pacing in front of me, staring me down.

Flashback to Troy's fist wrapped around the screwdriver handle.

Aleesa Desca.

We do this all the time, Dr Jess and I, back and forth. Nice and comforting, then a hit to the guts. She knows I say things just to get at her, just to hit her back. Slapping each other like fucking cartoon characters. She wants it to hurt, she wants to break me down, get through my defences. Reduce me to nothing and analyse the remains.

Connect the fucking dots.

Tick me off the list.

Dr Jess sits staring at me, calm, relaxed. Holds eye contact. It's part of their training. Show no emotion. Showing emotion could affect the response of the patient, distort the diagnosis. So Dr Jessica Snowden sits, back straight, blank face. Staring. Her hair's not tied up today, blonde and dried out, straight down past her shoulders. Red lipstick. Better looking than normal, today.

'What about her?' I ask. Interlocked fingers means you're tense.

'Didn't you have a thing with Aleesa Desca?' Dr Jessica Snowden dumbs down her language to show we're on the same page. To show that she understands me.

'No,' I say, concentrate on my movements.

'Nothing?' Dr Jess asks, taps her pen on her notepad.

Close your eyes and you're stressed.

'No,' I say.

Dr Jessica Snowden raises her eyebrows. She wears contact lenses some days and you can see the thin outline of them around her eyes. She puts her head down, writes notes, and I move my eyes all around real quick, try to get them ready to stay still again. Look in any direction and it means something to Dr Jess. She has dark roots to her blonde hair, starting to show along her hairline.

'Are you married?' I ask.

Dr Jessica Snowden lifts her head to face me again, holds her left hand up, palm facing her chest.

'No, I'm not.' She smiles.

'You know,' I tell her, 'psychologists often end up sleeping with their patients.' Look her up and down. 'Happens all the time.' My eyes halt, staring at her tits.

Dr Jessica Snowden shifts her body, looks at her watch.

'That's it for today then,' she says, sounding more bored than intimidated.

I'm thinking of her reading over my rap sheet. Reading about Rohypnol and Mrs Arthur and everything that went wrong. I tell her this could be the start of something beautiful.

'This is not helping,' Dr Jessica Snowden says.

'You never know,' I say.

She opens the office door, waits for me to walk out.

'This'll be easier if you work with me,' she says.

'Bye, Jess.' I give a cute, fingers up and down wave. 'See you next time.'

I wake up on Thorley's third-floor balcony, the polished stone against my face and the sounds of cars whispering past the city buildings. My phone is ringing. It could have been ringing for hours. Someone has thrown a sleeping bag across my legs, cold and wet with the early morning air. It's still dark, music playing inside, muffled behind the glass sliding door. Cars washing through the streets below.

And my phone is ringing, rattling against the tiles. It's fucking 4 am.

'I think I've killed him,' Troy panics down the line.

Thorley has told me about Troy's steroid rage, how sometimes he goes nuts, destroys anything near him, be it human or not. Thorley told me about the time Troy brought down a bus stop, then threw its framework remains at a passing car, like he was fucking King Kong taking down the city. He's normal one minute, then breathing fire the next. Thorley told me to get the fuck away if I see it coming. It's in his eyes, apparently.

86

And Troy's spitting down the line. 'I think I killed him. Seriously,' he says.

I tell the big fuck to slow down, and he tells me he fucked some girl he met at a nightclub then got in a taxi to go home. He tells me the taxi driver didn't speak English and how it's bullshit that immigrants can just come over here and get our jobs.

Troy says the cabbie took him for a ten-minute trip, ten fucking minutes, he says, and then he asked Troy for fifty dollars. The big fuck told the cabbie to fuck off, gave him a twenty and opened the door. The driver got out of the car, started yelling at Troy, grabbing at his pockets, asking for his money, said he'd call the police and Troy went to walk away but the taxi driver blocked him. The taxi driver pulled out a mobile phone, started pushing buttons.

This is when I imagine Troy's eyes turn steroid-rage red. Like the fucking Hulk.

Troy says the driver grabbed him and the big fuck gripped the cabbie's face, his veins pumping rage to his brain. Troy held onto the guy's jaw, tried to crush his face with his grip. Troy held the taxi driver's face and rammed his other fist into his nose. Troy says he felt the cabbie's nose break, squash underneath his knuckles.

The taxi driver fell to the footpath, hit his head on the gutter. But the big fuck, the chemicals in his veins, he wasn't done. Troy dragged the half-conscious man back to the footpath, dropped his body. The cabbie lying on his back in the moonlight, the engine of the cab still running. Troy stomped at the cabbie's rib cage, punched at the guy's mouth, made sure he knocked some teeth out. The taxi driver's eyes rolled back and Troy could feel raindrop speckles of blood. Then he realised what he'd done.

The big fuck sees the cab driver's blood spattered on the concrete of the footpath, a stray tooth caught in the cabbie's beard, shining under the moonlight. The big fuck ran, ran straight into his house, peeking out from behind the front curtain. The taxi driver lying, unmoving, just outside the glance of the cab's headlights, the engine still whistling.

Then Troy calls me. He calls me because he thinks I know how to deal with this stuff. Because he knows I broke a kid's fingers with a hammer one time.

'I think I've seriously killed him,' he says. 'I hit him in the fucking temple, man. He's still just lying there.'

Imagine the big fuck hiding in his lounge room, peeking through a gap in the curtains, then sliding down into the security of his pillow fort.

'Oh, fuck,' he says. 'What do I do?'

I take Thorley's car, drive through the city streets, deserted and quiet, shining from the rain. Troy meets me outside his house, clutching his mobile phone. He looks up and down the street, dark and lonely in the night. Traffic lights change in the distance down the straight road. No taxi in sight.

'It was here,' Troy points to the footpath. Some blood, or maybe something else, is spilled across the concrete.

'Well, what happened?'

'He's fucking gone,' Troy rubs at his white hair in confusion, turns his hands palms up.

I don't know what he's taken tonight.

'Must've gone home,' I tell him, pissed off that he's dragged me out for nothing.

'Or the police picked up the body.' Troy replies.

'You big – ' I stop myself in time for a car to flash by, a red P-plate on the windscreen. The car slows down beside Troy and I, some kid leans out.

'Hey, you fucking having a lovers' tiff, are ya?' The kid slurs, his words slipping on the alcohol which floods his brain. 'Fucking . . .' The kid can barely focus on us, his eyes half-looking at us, half-looking past. His friends laugh and yell from inside the car and they speed off down the street.

'Fuck,' Troy yells, echoing past the houses and parked cars. 'I gotta fucking sleep.'

'Wait,' I say, watching the P-plate car's red brake lights drifting across to the wrong side of the road and back again. It slows for the traffic lights in the distance.

'Get in the car,' I tell Troy.

Thorley came up with the rules. He'd written them in thick black whiteboard marker, scribbled across his glass coffee table.

'After Adelaide,' he tells me, 'we need to be more careful.'

The first rule is: 'Never use your real name.'

Thorley had sat up all night going over his regulations, revising what he needed to say. He told me once how he spent nights sitting on the roof of his building, smoking and watching the traffic flow along the veins of the metropolis and out across the West Gate Bridge. Listening to the hum of the Arts Centre spire, its brilliant blue light flooding the night sky all around. Reminds me of the fluorescent blue of city toilets and night buses that makes it harder for the drug addicts to locate their veins. Thorley sat listening to the distant whispers of the streets below and going over his rules.

Apparently, Thorley didn't sleep most nights.

Instead of your name, Thorley says, use the names of celebrities. He says we should pick the first name of a modern celebrity and the surname of an old one. Modern celebrities have names more common to modern society, but old celebrities had more classic, traditional, believable surnames. Like, for instance, Brad Pitt and Rod Stewart – Brad Stewart. Matt Damon and Errol Flynn – Matt Flynn. These are names people will not question, and there will be no time wasted trying to come up with a clever alias.

The second rule, in half-joined block letters, is: 'Always have a Second.'

'If you weren't with us in Adelaide, Harris would have been busted,' Thorley tells me. 'Harris would have talked to the cops and he would have told them everything. Then we'd be fucked.'

There has to be a Second, always, someone with you to keep an eye on the surroundings. A sort of safety net. A Second will step in if he notices anything, like a security guard or – more often – a nosy, jealous friend, tagging along watching everything their pretty friend does. The Second is to watch for this and work as a distraction if necessary. Distraction can be anything from starting conversation with the ignored friend to blunting your fists on the nosy friend's face. We usually took the second option if it was a nosy guy hanging around a target. I remember Uncle stomping the feet of a bar stool onto one nosy friend's forehead. He went too far that time.

The Second also has to look out for randoms who may notice something's up. Anything goes wrong, and the Second needs to step in before we get busted.

'One of them goes down and we're all fucked,' Thorley tells me.

Third rule: 'Be wary of ethnicity.' Racial background plays a big part in target selection. Avoid Asian girls, for starters. Asian families tend to have lots of relatives in close clusters and they will all become soldiers if you upset the family nest. 'Like ants,' Thorley explains. They tend to carry knives and they will not fight fair. The risk of being seen leaving with an Asian girl by somebody who knows her is too high, especially in the city.

Also, be aware of Croatians, Turks and Greeks. These communities are close-knit and will hunt you down if they find out you've had anything to do with hurting their sister/cousin/relative. Australians tend to be more defeatist, resigned to their fate. More willing to accept that revenge is futile. 'Two wrongs don't make a right' mentality. Tourists, Americans, English – all fine. But always be wary of ethnicity.

Fourth rule: 'Leave immediately.' Once you have your target, you do not hang around out the front of the nightclub letting their security cameras get solid images of you. Do not walk to the 7-Eleven down the street. Do not go to another place. You are not on a date. If possible, the Second should have a car waiting out the front ready to go. Once you have your target, you get out and into the car. This measure is aimed at avoiding questions, avoiding cameras. CCTV is fucking everywhere these days. Try to avoid using cabs for this same reason.

Fifth rule: 'No evidence.' This means no obvious signs, no bruises or cuts. They wake up with a headache and a jagged, kaleidoscope memory of something, but nothing else. No marks, no broken bones. 'Avoid bruising of the inner thighs if you can,' Thorley says.

Sixth rule: 'She does not stay over.' Under no circumstances does a target stay the night. Take her back to where you found her, leave her at a taxi rank, a bench at a train station. A target cannot be dumped near your home, or taken back to their home. What if the worried father is sitting up in his lounge room waiting for her to get back, watching every car that comes down the street? Then you drive in and he gets a full view of your car, takes down the number plate. Then you're fucked.

No matter what, she must be gone before the sun comes up.

Seventh rule: 'No contact.' You do not contact a target afterwards, ever. No phone calls, no text messages, you leave if you see her walk into a place, you avoid her if you see her in the street. Imagine the deja vu she feels when she places your features into some memory but can't quite get it right. It is a one-night deal; never again. You do not make any type of contact for any reason.

Eighth rule: 'Don't talk.' Not ever. You do not talk to anyone about your weekend activities. There are five people who know about this, that is it. There will always be speculation and rumour. Never do we confirm or deny. What happens on a night stays on that night. You do not talk about it again.

I don't know exactly how Harris's parents got rich. What I do know is they loved westerns. Thorley and I had to go to Harris's house one time when Thorley said we needed cash. I asked, said: 'Don't you have money?' but Thorley didn't answer. Just smiled. Harris opens the door cautiously, peeking out to us.

'What's up, guys?' Harris says, meek.

'We're coming in,' Thorley tells him, pushes past and into the house.

The front room of Harris's home is bright white and huge, high ceilings, polished tiles and maintained grey carpets. Framed posters of Clint Eastwood and John Wayne films on the walls. Thorley leads the way through the front lounge room, through the kitchen, ignoring everything around him, storms down a darkened hallway and down a set of stairs, Harris tagging along behind us, saying nothing.

'You've gotta see this,' Thorley smiles to me, clinging on to the handles attached to a set of large, wooden double doors.

Thorley swings them open, grand entrance style. And through the double doors is a miniature old western town. Harris's entire backyard is dominated by this make-believe cowboy play set, real buildings you can walk into and use. A saloon dominates the scene, looming over a large in-ground pool. The ground is dry, dusty, a road leading past the general store, the jailhouse, two hotels (the 'Whorehouse' sign has been painted over and renamed).

Thorley leads me through, Harris, with his hands in his pockets, kicking the ground as he walks behind us. Thorley shows me the stable, saddles but no horses. The woodworking stall, carriage wheels half-built. Thorley takes a bottle from behind the bar in the saloon, empties it onto the wooden floorboards.

'Tell him about the bottles,' Thorley says to Harris, who keeps his head down as he speaks.

'They used to be full of alcohol, they changed it to water,' Harris says, deadpan.

'What the fuck is this?' I ask him.

'I used to love playing cowboys so my dad bought me a western town. He loves western films.' Harris rubs at the back of his neck as he speaks. 'My parents invite friends over for western theme nights and they watch shit like fucking *Pale Rider* and *The Wild Bunch* on a cinema screen overlooking the pool. They've got a projector and shit.'

Through the saloon window I can see a tyre-swing hanging off the noose beam at the end of the street.

'Harris hates it,' Thorley says, picking up a used bullet shell from the floor.

'Why?' I ask.

'It's fucking embarrassing. I've grown up playing in a frontier town. Every time someone comes over I have to explain this shit.'

'Shut the fuck up, Harris.' Thorley throws the shell at him, bounces off his T-shirt and clinks along the floor. 'We've come to get some cash from you,' Thorley tells him. 'We need money.'

'For what?'

'For spending. Go get the money.' Thorley looks pissed off, steps towards Harris.

'Harrison?' a woman's voice calls from outside, breaks the silence of the main street. 'Harrison, are you here?'

'Yes, Mum.'

Thorley walks over to the pool table, beside the stairs which have a broken rail. Maybe from a bar fight. A drum kit and an unplugged video arcade machine are crowded into the corner of the room.

'Harrison, I'm going out for lunch, do you want anything?'

'No, Mum.'

'Okay – bye, darling,' Harris's mother's voice trails off back into the house.

Thorley stands still for a moment, waiting to hear the doors close behind her. Points at Harris.

97

'You go inside now, and you get me some fucking money.'

Harris has his hands in his pockets, his head down. 'I don't know if he has any here.' Harris is upset, like a kid who doesn't want to clean his room.

Thorley snatches a pool cue from the table and rushes towards Harris, who takes his hands from his pockets quickly, holds them up in front of his face, starts stepping backwards. Thorley flips the cue around, getting the handle end ready to strike, stops just short of Harris, who's ducking his head into his body and saying 'sorry' over and over.

'You fucking . . . You go in there and get me the money. You know what the deal is.' Thorley speaks through his clenched teeth. 'You owe me.' Fakes like he's gonna hit him. Harris keeps his hands up to protect himself, shakes his head, gives a look like *Please don't make me do this*. Thorley winds the cue back a little more, his muscles tensed, ready to bring it down.

'I will fucking kill you, Harrison.' Thorley with both hands on the cue, holding it like a baseball bat. 'I'll show your parents the video.'

'Okay,' Harris says quickly, steps back away from Thorley. 'Okay, I'll go and look.' Harris leaves through the saloon doors, swinging behind him, goes back into the house. Thorley lowers the cue, walks back to the pool table, rests it down onto the green felt surface.

'What's the video?' I ask him.

Thorley ignores me, walks back through the saloon doors and out into the main street of western town.

*T*he New Punk is not about being a reasonable person. A responsible adult. Look at
them doing nothing. The responsible people. The
reasonable nobodies. Look at them. Surviving.
Working. Compromising. Look at them. The New
Punk is about never compromising, never a step
down. It's about getting in their faces, stepping
up. Doing what you have to. You don't have to
take shit from people like that.

You do not have to take that shit.

The New Punk is not about community
spirit. Helping your fellow man. Would it be
responsible for me to step in and help? Yes.
Would that person help me? No. Fuck them. You
can never guess what another person will do.
You can't bank on them catching you when you
fall. So they can't bank on you.

Fact: Assume the worst in people and you
will be right more often than wrong.

These people are not your friends.

Why would they be?

The New Punk is not about learning a better

way. Looking for meaning. You don't need it. You don't need forgiveness. I've heard all that shit before. That I can become a better person. That I can have a second chance. People will forgive me. But I don't want to live with that. Forgiveness. What sort of weak people would forgive me?

Fuck them.

The New Punk is not about spoilt fucking rich kids always getting everything they want, having it handed to them. Spoilt little rich girls planning their fucking white-wedding life from the time they can understand fairy tales. They have everything. They can have anything, anytime. Except now. Now they're on your time. You make the fucking rules.

You just take them.

Fuck them.

Dump them.

The New Punk is not about what your parents will think. What are they gonna do, stop speaking to you? Who gives a fuck?

MMum calls, sounds upset, shaky, says there's a family crisis, says I have to come home. Says: 'Please can you come home?'

Dad opens the front door for me, nods as I pass him. Mum's wearing a dress and Mum never wears dresses. She hugs me and I notice the new dining table. Mum holds my shoulders as she pulls back away. Her brown curly hair with strands of grey showing through.

'Your Nan is very sick. She's in the hospital,' Mum tells me, slowly, as if she's unsure how I'll take the news.

'Okay,' I say.

'We have to go to the hospital and visit Nan, then go back to Grandpa's place and help him out. All the family will be there.'

And my stomach sinks. Me, the family fuck-up, the one they talk to each other about on the phone, offer advice about. A fucking room full of disappointed people staring, judging me. I've stayed away from every family event for years for this exact reason.

I gesture to Dad, who's within earshot, say: 'Is he coming?'

The drive to the hospital is hot, quiet, radio announcer speaking shit. Family outings are not what they used to be. Mum doesn't dare say anything for fear of starting another fight. And Dad, I don't think he knows what to say. Driving patiently and slowly. The smooth ride of his BMW.

He loves that fucking car.

Hospital is bright, quiet. Peek in on people as we walk though the corridors. Families visiting sick relatives, crying. Patients watching high up, tiny TV sets from their beds. Some just lying, staring at the roof. Most of the patients, I can't even tell what's wrong with them. Nurses all smile whenever they pass. Me, looking at the equipment, looking at the drawers of coloured capsules and tablets. Looking for things we could use.

Nan is beeping, hooked up to hoses and pipes and she's asleep, not likely to wake up while we're here. I find a bench to lean on and wait for this to be over. Mum sits at Nan's side and holds her unconscious hand.

I'm thinking: *This is what the girls are like. This is how they are when we take them. Unconscious. Unaware of what's happening.*

Dad looks at Nan's medical chart like he has any idea, and Mum speaks to Nan, quietly so we can't hear what she's saying. Some guy with his arm in a sling in the bed next door, reading a magazine.

Nurse comes in, and she's old but she's fucking hot, white uniform, good tits, skinny legs. I imagine what she'd look like naked. The nurse moves around the bed, does checks on the various devices hooked up to Nan. Nurse looks up to me for a moment, and I'm imagining her lips around my cock. Me, trying to look cool, smiling at her. The nurse ignores me, blanks me completely, leaves the room, and when I turn back from checking her ass Dad is looking at me. Dad's staring at me.

Mum kisses Nan's hand and we leave, crowd into the elevator. Mum, she's crying quietly, trying not to let us notice, catches the tear sliding down her cheek. Dad puts a hand on Mum's back, between her shoulder blades. Me standing behind them as the lift doors open. My parents. Walking silently back to the car.

Grey, overcast day, the wind kicking up and blowing rubbish and loose bags up and around.

Look up at the gathering clouds through the sunroof as we drive.

Grandpa's house is busy, uncles and cousins and relatives I barely remember sitting on couches and working the kitchen, and kids playing all over the front lawn, behind Grandpa's tiny brick fence. Grandpa is sitting at the kitchen table, shakes my hand but doesn't look me in the eye. The scraping of cutlery against porcelain all through the room.

I find a spot to sit near the TV and hope this will all be over soon. Black-and-white midday movie playing. Pretend I'm watching as I try to listen in on conversations. Mostly just people saying 'yeah' and 'I know'.

Uncle Ian is one of my four uncles, married to my mum's sister. Ian is an older guy, was in the army then the police force then he retired. Ian also used to be a fucking drunk. Ian comes over to me, carrying a tiny plate with a piece of dark-brown cake on it in one hand, a spoon in the other. And when he sits down next to me I already know what he's going to do.

This has all been done before.

Ian settles beside me on Nan's floral-pattern couch, looks at me, waits for me to acknowledge him.

'How's school going?' Ian asks.

'Fine. All good.'

'Your mum tells me you've been getting in a bit of trouble.'

And I want to stop him before he does it, before he gets into the 'back in my day' bullshit. The 'in the army' bullshit. Ian, grey hair on the sides of his head, bald on top, he still looks pretty fit, pretty with it. I'm looking at his arms. I'm wondering if I could take him.

'I'm all good now, Uncle Ian. No problems.'

I wave a hand in front of myself. *Smooth sailing*.

'Come here,' Ian says, rests his cake onto the coffee table in front of us, waves me in closer.

Here it fucking comes.

Ian gets up near my face, so the grandkids on the carpet can't hear him. 'You need to stop fucking around, okay?'

I'm imagining Mum talking on the phone to my aunt, my aunt talking to Ian, asking him to have a word to me.

'Your mum is stressed out. She cries herself to sleep at night wondering what to do with you.'

I'm thinking: *Nice touch. I'm sure she does*. Feel Ian's hand grip onto the back of my neck, his fingers pushing in hard.

'You need to get your act together, mate, drugs and all that. You think you're tough? You think you know everything?'

It's Mr John Arthur all over again.

'When I was a cop we picked up kids like you every day. That's where you're headed, mate – to jail.'

The people who know better, always offering advice.

'It's no picnic in jail, you understand that?'

This has all been done before. I have to stop him. Fuck this.

'Fuck off, Ian,' I say.

The kids on the carpet stop pushing their toy trucks and swinging their teddy bears and look up, eyes wide.

Ian moves back, staring straight at my face, anger rising. His ears going bright-red. The vein in his forehead ready to explode.

And right there, the kids all looking up at us, the relatives, my Grandpa, I get right up in his face: 'Fuck you.'

Ian is shocked, looks around the room, his hand still gripping hard on my neck, looks at my face, his eyes intense. And I punch him, hit Ian right in the jaw, hear my fist crack against his cheek. Ian looks surprised, amazed, still holding my neck and I punch him again, once to the side of the head in the same spot, then another, a direct uppercut with my left, snap his fucking mouth shut, hear his teeth clash together. And Ian, he was in the army but that was a long time ago.

My other uncles rush over, grab hold of us before Ian can hit back, his fist red and ready to fight. He has an uncle on each arm, dragging him away. One uncle pushes me up out of my chair and against the mantelpiece, photos of my relatives all across it, knocking them over. My father steps in between us, stares Ian down.

'He hit me,' Ian yells. 'That little shit.' And Ian looks around after he says 'shit'.

His wife, my aunty, she does a long blink, puts down her wine glass, looks around the room. Looks for what her husband has been drinking.

Ian has his mouth open, but no idea what to say here, stares at his wife, shaking his head. My uncle, whichever one it is, he loosens his grip on me when I don't fight back but keeps a hand on my shoulder, holds me against the mantelpiece as he moves away.

I put my hands up, blood pulsing through me. My knuckles burning. Mum rushes over. 'What's wrong? What happened?'

I keep staring at Ian, who's staring at me, rage in his eyes, vein about to burst from his head. Bright red marks where I hit his face, almost glowing. I smile at him.

Mum puts her hands either side of my head, pulls my face down to look me in the eye. 'What's going on?' She's upset, tears ready to leak out any moment.

'Nothing,' I tell her. 'It's okay, Mum.'

'It's not okay.'

'It is okay.'

'What are you doing?' Mum cries.

'Nothing, Mum. I'm sorry.' Stare back at Ian. That fuck.

'Say you're sorry to Ian,' Mum screams at me, the tears flowing now.

'Fuck him.'

And Mum smacks my shoulder, her teeth gritted. She's trying to hit hard.

'I'm sorry to you, Mum,' I say, put my hands on her shoulders, look at her eyes. Tears rolling down her face.

Dad stands behind her, looking at me, unsure what to say. Aunties, cousins, Grandpa, all staring. Mum crying harder, grabbing onto my shirt.

The fuck-up of the family.

'I'm gonna go, Mum,' I tell her.

'Where?' she whimpers, barely able to say the word, saliva threads connecting her lips.

'I'm sorry, Mum. I'll come back home soon.'

Dad looks at me, like he wants to talk, but says nothing.

'I'm sorry,' I say to him.

Mum holds onto my arm, my hand, my fingers. Till I'm out of her reach.

Catch the next train back to the city.

There's a guy at the train station, standing in front of me, staring at me when I walk up, and I'm wondering if I could take him, if he got up in my face right now. He's about thirty, shaved head, wearing tracksuit pants and an old Nike T-shirt, tucked in, the logo cracked and the colours faded. Thin gold chain around his neck. White sneakers that look too big for his skinny legs. He checks the vending machine for abandoned change, scrapes his fingers through the coin return. Paint specks across his worn hands. The guy leans up onto the fence, mumbles something at me.

Announcement comes over: *The next train to depart will be the four-fifteen to Flinders Street.*

The train pulls up and I walk along to make sure I get on to the same carriage as the tracksuit guy, and he smiles when he sees me step on board, lets me walk past him. Maybe I could have got onto the next carriage. But fuck him. Tracksuit guy says something I can't understand, takes a seat near the door. Inside my jacket pocket, I roll my fingers into a fist as I pass him.

And right up the back, sitting with her head rested against the rear wall of the carriage, in the seats where drunk guys go to piss and throw up and no-one ever sits there, right there is Aleesa, dressed nice, make-up, perfect straight hair, staring out the window. She has a black short-sleeve top on that plunges at the neck and shows off her tits, short denim skirt. Aleesa has her knees together, hands rested in her lap, white handbag on the seat next to her.

I walk towards her as the doors beep closed and the train pulls out. Aleesa flashes her eyes towards me, looks me up and down, then smiles.

'Well, look who's here,' she says.

'Hi. We've met before, right?' I ask, smiling.

'How's the rape squad going for you?'

And I stop breathing for a moment when she says this, look around to see if anyone heard.

'No-one heard,' Aleesa says. 'What are you doing?'

'Nothing. Had to go home to get some stuff.'

Aleesa moves her bag. 'You can sit with me but if you start to bore me I may have to ask you to leave,' she says.

Sit down beside her, right up close, our legs touching, side to side. Aleesa smiles, looks at my face.

'Are you stalking me?' she asks.

'No. I had no idea you'd be on the train. What are the chances?' I say, smiling. 'Where are you going to?'

'Boyfriend's place.'

Hearing her say this hurts more than I expected.

'You have a boyfriend?'

'Maybe.' And she holds eye contact. Soft skin. Black eyeliner that seems to connect with her dark eyes.

'Well, you just said you do.'

'You're boring me already,' Aleesa says, turns to look out the window, the suburbs flashing by.

'Are you going out tonight?' I ask, but Aleesa doesn't answer, keeps staring away from me. The sunlight reflecting off her shining lips. They look glossy, wet.

'I enjoyed fucking you the other night,' I tell her.

Aleesa turns her head back to me, smiles, perfect white teeth.

'Really?' she asks, her eyebrows raised.

'Yeah.'

'Well, that's a good thing,' Aleesa tells me, pats my leg as she speaks. 'See, it's good to actually meet a girl and not have to spike her drink to take her home with you.'

I flinch a little when she brings it up again, like I didn't need the reminder.

Aleesa fakes a look of concern. 'Oh, it's okay,' she says, grabs my face with one hand, fingers either side of my chin. 'You're much better looking than the rest of those losers,' she says, pouts at me as she squeezes my cheeks.

'I don't do it,' I tell her through my pushed-together lips. Aleesa smiles.

'Of course you don't.' And she lets go of my face.

'You said everybody knows?' I ask.

Aleesa, looking through her small bag, nods in response. 'Everybody,' she says. 'Just be careful of that guy you're hanging out with.'

'Who? Thorley?'

Aleesa nods, checks her phone for messages.

'He's clever, he's . . .' And she trails off as her attention diverts to her phone, her finger moving fast across the keypad.

'What?' I ask.

Aleesa looks up to me. 'There's just something not right about him.'

'How do you know so much?'

Aleesa puts her phone back into her bag, zips it up, drops it into her lap. She looks at my eyes, puts her hand up to my face and I haven't shaved this week, can feel her fingers across my stubble.

Aleesa leans in and kisses me, opens her mouth, pushes her tongue over mine. I rest my hand onto the side of her neck. Breathe in her perfume. Our teeth connect as the train bumps. Then she pulls away, leans back against the carriage wall.

Aleesa slides her fingers along my arm, down my palm. Slides them in between my fingers, holds on to my hand. She leans her head on my shoulder as the train rocks further along,

113

past the streets, the houses. Backyards, clotheslines spinning in the afternoon breeze. The orange sunlight haze of the afternoon making me squint. Streetlights switching on as the day fades. Kids playing cricket in the street. And I don't want to move. Don't want to speak for fear of fucking this up.

The smell of her hair.

Aleesa stands up as the train eases into the station, pulls her hand away from mine, straightens her skirt, pulling it from side to side and bending her legs, one at a time. She looks at my face again, smiles.

'Where are you going?' I ask.

'I told you already.'

'We could go somewhere else.'

Aleesa laughs, lingers in front of me for a moment. Then walks away. I watch her as she disappears through the sliding doors of the station and walks out along the exit ramp. She doesn't look back as the train pulls away. But she's smiling.

The carriage is empty except for me and the tracksuit guy. The fuck. He's staring at me, his feet up on the chair in front of him, smoking a cigarette. The mist of the smoke drifting through the sunlight all around him. He says something that I can't make out, stares as he sucks another drag. An empty beer bottle rolls from side to side in the aisle. Tracksuit guy smiles, looks out the window.

I can still smell Aleesa around me. Still feel her fingers between mine. The train carrying me towards the city.

The lights in the carriage stutter and buzz into life.

Uncle meets me at the next station, leaning up on some family van piece of shit in the car park, broken headlight and crack down the middle of the windscreen. I don't ask if this is his car.

'How were the parents?' Uncle is smiling, smoking, arms crossed.

I watch the train pull out, look back to Uncle. 'There was some guy on the train,' I tell him.

'What guy?'

'Just some dude, staring at me and saying shit.'

'What did he say?' Uncle stands up, looks interested.

'Just when I was getting off, he'd been staring at me on the train, then when I got out he was like, "Yeah, walk away, faggot."'

'What did you do back?' Uncle asks.

'Nothing, I was getting off the train.'

'Did you say anything?'

I shake my head.

Uncle drops his cigarette onto the concrete of

the car park, swings around, opens the van door.

'Get in the van,' he says.

We drive through the backstreets, Uncle pushing the old van to its limits, over-revving it on corners and through roundabouts, swinging us from side to side. In the back, something hits the wall and makes a metal-on-metal sound. Uncle accelerates into the car park of the next train station, pulls it to a halt, cranks on the hand brake.

'Let's go,' he says, picks up a red steering lock from behind his seat and gets out the door quick, rushing towards the stairs, up to the crossover bridge. Me a step behind, trying to keep up.

Announcement comes over, echoes through to us running along the platform. Train approaching.

'Which carriage?' Uncle asks as the train pulls in.

'The second.'

And Uncle looks back at me, raises his eyebrows, lifts his chin.

'Second,' I repeat.

The train hisses to a halt and we rush through the doors of the carriage, the tracksuit guy alone, leaning up against the window. He looks at Uncle, storming towards him, then at me, recognises me straightaway, goes to get up but it's too late.

Uncle is up on him, swings the steering lock, hits the guy across the head, the guy's face bounces off the window. The doors beep closed and the train moves away from the station. Track-suit guy puts his arms up over his face, kicks his legs and Uncle grabs the guy's ankles, pulls him further over the chair in front, slides his body down, his head now on his seat. Uncle keeps swinging with the steering lock, connects with the tracksuit guy's elbow, his ribs, his chest, belts at the guy's fingers covering his head. Uncle hits him in the ribs to make him shift his focus, waits for him to move his hands away from his face, then smashes the metal into his mouth.

The guy is yelling, screaming, not words. Uncle has a psychopathic look in his eyes, his teeth gritted together tight. Swinging the steering lock over and over, like he's hacking into this guy's body with each blow.

Then we stop, the tracksuit guy crying and puffing, huddled into the corner, sitting on the floor of the carriage, his head leaning on the seat. One hand wavering in front of his face to shield any more hits. There's blood coming from his eye, smeared across his face. Blood in his hair.

Uncle stands up, riding the unsteady motion of the train. Announcement comes over for the next station. Tracksuit guy covers his face with his hands. The train slows into the station and I rush back to the other end of the carriage, grab the empty beer bottle from the aisle. Uncle pulls the doors open and I run back, throw the bottle at the tracksuit guy's face as I pass him, bouncing it off his fingers and knocking his head back against the wall. Uncle holds the door open and we jump off, watch the train roll out into the darkness.

'You can't take shit from people like that,' Uncle tells me, breathing hard as he lights a cigarette. He looks at me, pats me on the back of the head. 'Fuck people,' he says.

We walk through the tunnel underneath the station, across to the opposite platform, catch the next train back to Uncle's van.

'Why do they call you Uncle, man?' I ask.

Uncle smiles, raises his eyebrows as he takes a long drag, the orange glow lighting up his face, the stubble of his shaved head.

Thorley comes out of his room holding a walkie talkie in one hand, other hand pushing an earpiece in. He concentrates on what he's hearing, walks over to me on the balcony, looking out along the traffic in the night. The chain of headlights along the street reminds me of Christmas. Thorley's eyes switch up to mine.

'Some guy's died, fucked himself up at the Casino.' Thorley throws the radio at the table, but misses and it falls to the floor. He rushes back to his room to get his jacket. 'C'mon, man, let's check this out.'

Police cars are crowded around the Casino entrance, officers in long dark jackets and blue shirts writing notes and talking on mobile phones. The body is covered with a grey blanket, but the blood is still all across the footpath, kids from the nearby video arcade looking scared and holding onto each other.

What's happened is the guy has punched through a window. The guy has smashed it then cut his artery on the glass as he followed through, ripping along the vein. The guy's then walked back around the footpath, back towards the Casino entrance, and fallen to the concrete. Died of massive blood loss, probably less than a minute after cutting his vein.

I'm thinking: *This guy, he's a strong guy, strong enough to punch straight through glass, like he's seen in the movies.* I'm thinking: *This guy, not for one second did it cross his mind that it would be the last thing he would ever do.*

Thorley is moving his head to see between the gaps in people surrounding the body, security guards with plastic numbers hanging from their jackets and distant, uncaring looks.

A police officer comes through from behind us, red and blue lights flashing all around. The officer and his partner, they push through the crowd to get into the crime scene, push past Thorley.

'Thanks, cunt-stable,' Thorley says at the man's back.

The officer stops, turns back around. 'Oh, you're a real bright spark, aren't you, mate?' He steps right up close to Thorley. 'Why are you here?'

'Wanted to see the dead body,' Thorley answers quickly, without flinching.

The officer reaches for his notepad, the other officer standing close behind. 'What's your name, mate?'

'Ben Wilder,' Thorley answers without a second's hesitation. Thorley stands up, stares the officer down.

The officer doesn't write anything on the notepad, maintains eye contact with Thorley.

'Well, Ben Wilder, do you know the deceased?'

'No.'

'Were you a witness to the crime?'

'No.'

'Then fuck off.' The officer spits the words at Thorley's face.

Thorley smiles, looks down at the officer's feet, rolls his eyes back up to the guy's face. Laughs to himself.

'No problem, cunt-stable.'

'What did you say?' the officer asks, leans in.

And I step in between them, say: 'Nothing', pulling Thorley back away from the crowd. 'He said nothing, mate, we're going.'

The officer stands waiting, watching us till we are out of his sight, me pulling Thorley back along the footpath.

'What the fuck are you doing, man?' I yell at him, dragging him across the busy street, the headlights bright on us.

'Fuck him,' Thorley says, and pushes my arms away, runs back towards the Casino entrance.

Thorley gets out ahead of me, runs further away, getting closer to the red and blue police lights, the small crowd around the body. I keep close enough to watch him, see him get up into the crowd, push through to the front. Thorley's head moves from side to side, looking for the officer and I catch up to him again, put a hand on his shoulder. Thorley quickly hits me away, gives me a 'don't you fucking stop me' look. Thorley keeps looking, scanning through the crowd, the blood, the body. A woman crying on the steps beside the dead man.

Thorley turns quickly, walks towards the police car, spits at the window. Thorley kicks at the back door, stomps his foot against the glass, but can't break it. He grabs at the flashing red light, tries to pull it away from the roof, breaks off the red cover. The small crowd is turning, looking at Thorley, who notices the sudden attention, stops, then runs off down the footpath. And I run to catch up.

Thorley, laughing and yelling, running along the city streets, not slowing up for a second. He divides couples walking side by side, dashes across in front of traffic, screams in the faces of strangers. Laughing. All the way back to the apartment.

Dr Jessica Snowden is running late, me reading through women's magazines, gossip columns, make-up advertisements. Pages smell like seven different kinds of perfume. Flip to a picture of Susannah Lockshardt smiling, close-up of her flawless lips. The image is repeated, smaller versions along the side of the page, each with a different shade of lipstick. Smiling. Turn the page quickly.

Dr Jess comes through, wearing black-framed glasses, hair tied back. She's lugging her black leather briefcase and carrying loose papers and apologising, asks me to come through to her office.

'Sorry,' she says. 'Car problems.'

'No problem.'

'It's always when you're already running late, isn't it?' Dr Jess says, unlocking her office door, tries to talk like we're friends. Like we're just hanging out.

She settles into her seat, rests her notes down on her large dark-wood desk. Clicks her pen three times, opens her book to a blank page.

'You know what?' Dr Jess says, just out of nowhere, as if this is off the record. 'I'm thinking about – '

'What was wrong with your car?' I cut her off. Dr Jessica Snowden says nothing for a moment, looks surprised.

'Ah, it was nothing, just had to get the guys to come out and get it started.'

'Okay,' I smile. 'I know a bit about cars, is all.'

Dr Jess turns her head to the notes in her lap, fingers through some loose pages.

'I've read through some of your notes, what you've written about . . .' Dr Jess says, scans through the notes in front of her, photocopies of my writing. 'Thorley,' she says. 'Have you heard from him since the arrests?'

I shake my head side to side, slowly. 'Why were you hanging around with Thorley?'

'He was a friend of mine.'

'But didn't you think "This isn't right?" Why get involved with this?'

I look around Dr Jess's office, the neat bookshelves, wooden frames around her certificates. Sunlight coming through the grey-coloured blinds. Dr Jessica Snowden is watching my every move, everything means something. Put your hands on top of your head and you're surprised. Look to your right and you're lying. Every motion, every action, Dr Jess is noting.

Everything means something.

'Your car's all right, now?' I ask.

'It's fine.'

'Thorley was on my side. Do you understand?' I tell Dr Jessica Snowden, look at her hand, her silver pen ready to note down everything.

'But why would you believe that?' Dr Jess says.

'I know him.'

'Did you know he was using everyone around him?'

'He wasn't.'

'Think about it. Troy. Harris. Uncle.'

Dr Jess stops to let her words sink in, watches for any movement, any reaction. If I move my hands, cross my legs.

'What did he want you for?' Dr Jess asks. Straight-faced. Calm.

I smile at her. 'What was wrong with your car, Jess?'

She doesn't move, keeps still, staring. Crosses her hands over each other.

'Someone broke into my car, smashed the driver-side window,' Dr Jess says, frustration in her voice.

'I know some people who might know who did it. Where do you live at?'

Dr Jess doesn't change her expression, stares straight at me.

'What makes you think you were any different to the other guys?' she asks again.

'Give me your phone, Jess, and I'll call around

right now, see if I can find out who tried to steal your car.'

'Forget about my car. It's fine. Why were you any different from them?'

'Give me the phone, Jess?' I say, holding my hand out to her.

Dr Jessica Snowden speaks louder, more forceful. 'You were no different,' she tells me. 'He was using you too.'

'Maybe you're right, Jess,' I say, smiling. 'You're smarter than I am.' Reach over to her desk, pick up a thick, leather-bound book, open it, tear out a page, screw it up. Throw it across the room. It bounces and rolls along the mat, into the wall.

'What does that mean, Jess?' I ask. 'You analysing this? You taking notes?' Hold her stare.

'Put the book back, please,' Dr Jess says.

I spit onto the open page in front of me, close the book back up, push it together tight. Put it back up onto her desk.

'Write your notes,' I tell her.

Imagine grabbing her hair and pulling her over the desk.

'You're much smarter than me, Jess,' I say.

School, classes, kids in ties and jackets, school emblem on the chest, and then Troy is up in my face, holding his phone up in front of me, saying: 'Check this out.' On the screen there is a photo of a girl smiling, naked except for her black panties. She's pulling a black skirt up over her knees. Or maybe taking it off. She has long dark hair and big puffy lips.

'How fucking hot is this chick? Wait . . .' Troy says, fumbles with the buttons on his phone for a second, turns the screen back round to me.

Same girl, now naked, her right hand over her left tit, arm covering her nipples. Her other hand on her hip, her mouth open slightly. Troy's hand is shaking as he holds it up for me. 'And this is the best.'

Troy pulls the phone away, presses buttons again, beeping in his hand, holds the screen up in front of me. It's a video, grainy, unsteady, the girl fucking someone, sitting up on some guy's cock. She runs her hand through her hair then slides it down her face, her fingers catching on her lips.

The video has been taken by the person she is riding, the guy she is fucking. The video is of Troy. The girl bounces up and down, moans, flicks her hair. She smiles at the camera, says: 'You are not recording this, are – ' And the video cuts out.

'How good is that?' Troy says, excited.

'Yeah. She's hot. So you actually picked this chick up, straight up?' I ask.

'I don't like to use that shit all the time, yeah?' Troy flexes his arm muscle, massive, holds it up for me to see. 'Check that shit out, man.' Troy rolls his fist to see the muscles move around his arm, the veins raised up to the surface. 'Like a fucking python wrapped around my arm.' And Troy nods, staring at his bicep, a serious look on his face.

'How long you spend in the gym to get like that?' I ask, and Troy stands up tall, like I've picked a topic he's happy to get into.

'Five days a week, man. I used to be a skinny little kid, stick arms'. Troy smiles, crooked teeth. 'I used to be . . . like you.' He laughs, squeezes my arm, then lets go.

'The steroids'll help that,' I say, and Troy looks down at the floor, puts a hand on the back of his head. The question about his shrunken balls is right there, right about to come out of my mouth.

Troy looks up at me. 'I don't take steroids.' And he stares. Blank. 'Don't ever say that to me again.'

'Okay, man.'

Troy keeps staring.

'She's hot,' I say, pointing to the phone in his hand.

He smiles again, looks back at the screen. Nods. He puts on some fake eastern European accent to speak: 'When I was little man like you, maybe I would have to spike drink all time. But now I am big man.' And Troy flexes his muscles again, looks like he's stretching his shirt, about to rip through the fucking fabric. 'Ladies love that, yes?'

I nod to him.

'This lady' – he points to his phone – 'one time I am fucking her over couch' – and he grabs an imaginary set of hips, humps the air – 'and her parents, they come home.' Troy waves, smiles, acting out his reaction to her mum and dad's sudden arrival. 'She love the cock, this lady. Maybe you see her sometime, yes?'

'Maybe, man.'

'I give number to Thorley.' Troy points at me, continues with the accent. 'Good fuck,' he says, holds a fist up in front of himself, shakes it. 'You have good time.'

Troy breaks back to his normal accent. 'Oh, hey, have you seen those fucking rules Thorley has written?'

'Yeah.'

'What's up with that? Rules?' Troy shrugs. 'What happened to you dickheads in Adelaide?'

One day I found Thorley cross-legged and naked on his kitchen floor. He told me he hadn't slept for four days. What he was doing was sharpening a pin, sharpening it on a grey pebble. Thorley told me he was going to use it to stab the fly and he waved his finger in the air, as if to say 'It's around here some place'.

'Like this,' he says, poking at the air. He smiles at me, his eyes like carved red holes in his flesh.

'Let's be truck-drivers,' he declares, as if it's the greatest suggestion he's ever made.

Thorley quickly dresses himself and leads the way out the front door. His plan for us to be truck-drivers is based around taking massive amounts of Duromine and driving a rental van to Queensland to deliver nothing to nobody. He tells me this as we walk down the street, Thorley squinting at the sunlight and staring everybody down. He goes quiet whenever people pass us on the footpath, as if his information is top secret and maybe they're spies.

Thorley rents a van, uses a fake ID with the name Ethan Wells, and saddles up into the driver's seat, runs his hands round the steering wheel. The rental van smells like lemon and has thin paper welcome mats on the floor. In the back of the van, Thorley has packed one single grey plastic crate, strapped it down with ropes. In the crate are bottles of tequila and pills of every colour and shape. Thorley narrows his eyes, looking out at the traffic.

'Here's the fucking story,' he says, without taking his focus off the cars and buses passing by. 'We're working for Hamilton's, a huge logistics company. Someone has called in and said he needs a package on his desk in Queensland by nine o'clock tomorrow morning, and our manager at Hamilton's, he's getting his nuts busted by the company chief, who is getting *his* nuts busted by the shareholders. So the company chief, not wanting to lose this valuable client, says he can do it. But he can't, not when you factor in breaks and shift allowance.'

Thorley shakes his head. 'And that's where we are. We've just taken out a massive loan for our truck, we have to make the delivery on time or we won't get the next job and we'll have to take our kids out of school and live in the back seat of the family car, get me? So we have to drive all night. We can't fucking stop till we get there.' He shakes his head again, straight-faced.

'You scared?' Thorley asks as he starts the engine, revs once, twice.

I tell him no.

'I haven't slept for four days,' he says. 'You scared?' He smiles to me, mad-man style, his eyes dug back into his head, trying to escape the daylight and rest.

Again, I tell him no.

'Don't be.'

He rams the gearstick into place and double-jolts out and into the traffic. I look back at the other rental cars lined up, white-clean, waiting to be driven.

And I'm thinking: *This van ain't never coming back here.*

'We're fucking truck-drivers,' Thorley yells to nobody, swallowing down a grey and brown tablet and spitting onto the cars beside us.

After five hours on the road, and Thorley occasionally driving at oncoming traffic 'just to scare them away', we pull into a truck-stop. By this time the sun has disappeared. Somehow neither of us had noticed till we got out and into the night air. We stagger through the service-station shop, the shitty fluoro lights sucking the colour from Thorley's skin, making him look like paper. He pokes his chest out whenever we pass a real truck-driver, flashes his Duromine pills at them.

Thorley strides up to one guy, some old trucker wearing a dirty cap and a red and black plaid winter jacket. The guy has big knuckles covered in tiny scratches. Grey flecks of hair in his dirty, five-day beard. Thorley offers him a tablet, tells him they'll keep him going all night.

'We'll fuck them up,' Thorley whispers to me. 'We're fucking truck-drivers'.

We lean on each other to stop ourselves falling onto display stands of chips and plastic-sealed magazines. Then we stumble back into the cold night air.

Thorley steps into a running pace, dashes over to a line of parked cars and trucks.

'This is us right?' he asks me, points to a large refrigeration truck.

I suddenly feel crippled with paranoia, worried one of the real truck-drivers is going to catch us near their prime-movers, their Macks. Movies have taught me truck-drivers love their trucks. I tell Thorley it's not ours, yell a whisper at him.

Thorley climbs into the truck, his legs disappearing inside the cabin. The engine rumbles and shakes to life. I run to the passenger side door of the refrigeration truck, jump in to stop him. Thorley stares at me as I climb up to his side, his face blank and straight.

'Did you bring the package?' he asks.

I run back to the rental van, rip the grey crate from the back, cradle it back to the refrigeration truck. And we drive out onto the highway, the tequila like acid down my thieving throat.

Thorley whispers song lyrics to himself as the refrigeration truck hums along the road at night, the white lines rolling beneath us, the pace of a heartbeat. The cabin is cluttered with papers, ripped-open envelopes, boxes of Panadol. There's a photo of a man and a woman near my feet, underneath a screwed-up paper bag.

I turn down the white noise of the CB radio to listen, open the window to feel the night breeze as it runs through the trees that rise up into the darkness beside the road. I can see it brush by each individual leaf and branch on its way towards the stars, makes me smile. And from whatever I've taken, whatever is sifting through my bloodstream, Thorley's song sounds beautiful and simple. My breaths seem to last forever, the vibration of the truck feels like levitation.

I tell Thorley we're nearly there, but he doesn't respond, his eyes shut already. And the truck drifts along the straight road.

I remember hearing a car horn moan through my dream and into the real world. Tyres shrieking against the asphalt. Then everything braking, hard. The roadside posts and grass turned upside-down, spinning past the window of the refrigeration truck. Dark shadows of the early morning, headlights bouncing like the torches of a search party. The roof bends, kicks into a V shape above me and everything loses sense and direction, glass in the air shattered into tiny granules of safe, squared-off diamonds.

Something splashes across my face and the seatbelt chokes against my ribs. Thorley's arms slam against the metal, the steering wheel closes in, up towards his chest. Thorley's mouth is open and his face looks like he is screaming but I can't hear him. Everything else is louder than I thought it would be. The refrigeration truck tumbles and splinters against the road. Something hits my chest, takes my breath. I try to see if the grey crate is okay but the seatbelt constricts to keep me upright. Then everything stops. Silence. The sound of a car engine idling somewhere off outside the bent-up cabin.

The road is by my face, liquid running across the asphalt. Chips of paint, glass splashed all over. Specks of blood. Thorley, his eyes closed, jerks to life suddenly, like a patient under the electric shock paddles. He's panicked, rushing to get out of the broken refrigeration truck as if it's a monster trying to swallow him. He brushes broken plastic and glass from his clothes, scrambles out and to his feet. I grab at my head, feel for blood. Two of my fingers are all bent up the wrong way against the dashboard, I can't move them.

When I untangle myself from the wreck I see Thorley, facing away from the truck, standing absolutely still, his pupils big as ten-cent coins. He stares at a flipped, busted-up hatchback car on its roof in front of us, its headlights still on, wheels still spinning. All around us is chaos, smashed across the roadway. A smear of shattered paint and tyre-marks.

My brain buzzes like a microwave, I can feel blood hissing and bubbling in my cerebellum. And Thorley runs across into an empty paddock, his back shifting to greyscale colours as he gets more distant in the darkness.

I only get close enough to the hatchback to see her body, all bent-up and broken. She is an older lady with tight curly hair. She's wearing blue tracksuit pants and a white T-shirt that says 'Dreamworld' on it. I only get close enough to see her face crying what looks like tears of pure blood from beneath her broken glasses. I get close enough to whisper, say: 'Are you okay?' Then I run after Thorley.

He's waiting for me to catch up and he grabs hold of me when I come past. Thorley, he has tears in his eyes.

'You fucking don't say anything to anyone,' Thorley spits through his clenched teeth.

Only then do I realise he has a split Coke can in his hand, he holds the thin aluminium to my face.

'I will kill you, you ever say anything.' Thorley pushes the sharp edge into my cheek, his breathing heavy. 'I will cut your fucking teeth out.' He has sweat all over.

I can feel the metal cutting, slicing into my

skin. Then he stops. Smiles. Pats at my head.

'You're all right, aren't you?' he asks.

I slowly nod to him, unsure what will come next.

'Let's get the fuck out of here.' Thorley runs ahead, dropping the broken can to the ground.

I feel at the cut on my face, the round-shaped slit pushed into my cheek. Blood rolls down my fingers.

The New Punk is not about friendship. No-one has your fucking back. No-one is there for you. We live in a road-rage society. And you are alone. You are not part of a team. We are not in this together. The New Punk is about not caring about anybody.

Not one bit.

And everybody knows. Fuck them all. Don't fear them – that's what they want. They smell it, like dogs. The New Punk is not about fear. Fear is fucking weak.

The New Punk is not about guilt. They rely on guilt. On shame. Just be normal. Just be like everyone else. The New Punk is about your rules. You are not like them. It's not about single-child syndrome. Attention-deficit disorder. It's not about your parents. They fucking gave you everything. The New Punk is your fault.

Note to psychologist: Analyse this.

The New Punk is smashed eye-sockets and blood-spattered shoes, and girls with one eye half-open jolting and shaking and being fucked,

fucked, fucked. Crying unconscious tears. Smearing make-up and vomit and blood. Is she dead? Is she dead? Then fuck her anyway, because we always get what we want. We always have what we want. This is what you are. This is your fault. And they all know.

The New Punk is all your fault.

The New Punk is not about love. What the fuck would you know about love? Why should anyone love you? Even for a second, for a moment. Why should she? Why can't they have just loved me? Fuck you. What the fuck do I care? Analyse this, Dr Jessica Snowden. Suck it down. Ask me again. Let me get to your pussy, Jess, and I'll show you what the New Punk is about. Let me spread your legs. Let me bend you over your desk and I'll show you. I'll hold your face down and get my fingers into your asshole while we fuck. I'll show you, I'll make you scream it. Leave you bleeding. Crying.

The New Punk is about no mercy.

The New Punk is about no fear.

Don't fucking look at me the way you are. I'd spit in your face as soon as speak to you. The New Punk is not about guilt. It is my fault and I deserve what's coming. You can't make me. You can't fucking make me. You are dead to me.

Take a breath.

Let's go cause some more damage.

Let's fuck some people up.

Fuck people.

Fuck them.
What do they know?
Analyse this, bitch.
The New Punk is about taking down every-
thing.

Uncle walks into Thorley's apartment at 3 am, leaves the door wide open behind himself, walks over to me, stands next to the couch. Me watching late-night music videos.

'Come with me,' Uncle says. 'I've got to show you something.'

Uncle leads the way along the city streets, walks with his head down, refuses to move aside for anyone. He bumps into a woman who is walking arm in arm with her husband, stumbles her off her high heels. Husband does nothing. Uncle bumps into a drunk teenager out the front of the Hungry Jack's, sending fries and a Coke flying. Uncle doesn't stop moving, doesn't look back. He leads me to a bridge over the Yarra River, climbs down the embankment, disappears into the shadows beneath.

Uncle is squatted down, fitting underneath the bridge, smiling at me as I come through to join him. He's nodding slowly, like he's listening to a drumbeat no-one else can hear.

'It's fucked up,' he says.

'What is?'

Uncle lifts his chin, gestures towards the water. And hanging from beneath the bottom of the bridge is a man. The man is swaying in the breeze, the rope creaking. The man is dead, his tongue hanging out, small marks of blood beneath the skin of his face. His eyes are wide and still, his skin pale. He has long hair that covers one of his eyes, wears a black long-sleeve shirt. There is a dark stain on the front of the dead man's jeans.

'I saw him do it,' Uncle says. 'I sat up in the darkness and watched him tie it up, then he let himself go and he shook. And I saw him regret it, watched the pain in his eyes as the tears were squeezed out of him, the blood to his brain stopping.' Uncle has a smile on his face, but it's not joy, it's forced. 'I watched the life go from him.'

And I don't know what to say here, watching the man hang in the night air, his joints all loose.

'The ambulance guys will take him down,' Uncle tells me.

'Did you call an ambulance?' I ask.

'I can't call them.' Uncle shakes his head, staring at the body, not looking away for a second.

'Who was he?' I ask.

'Some fuckhead,' Uncle replies, his voice deep, serious.

143

I see Uncle's shadow rocking back and forth out of the corner of my eye.

'That nearly happened to me once,' he says. 'I nearly died. My brother put a plastic bag over my head and held it there for ages.'

Uncle's eyes are red, but I can't tell if it is from crying.

'Did you know this guy?' I ask.

Uncle, still holding his forced smile, he nods, without ever looking away from the body. The rope creaking. Back and forth. The flames from the casino fire-cannons burst into the air, light up the dead man's features for a second. His eyes open, his neck squashed up. They fire again and I feel the heat wave push through to us as they light up the night. Fire reflected off the water, rising into the sky.

'It's fucked up, isn't it?' Uncle says, rocking back and forth, refusing to look away for a second.

After a while, Thorley and I didn't go to school every day. It became more of an optional activity. I started living at Thorley's house full-time, threw pillows at the couch to make it into my bed each night.

The two of us would wake up mid-morning, turn up late to classes. Just wander in, never apologising for our lateness. We'd stay up through the night watching failed American sitcoms and foreign movies with subtitles. We'd sit up on the roof of Thorley's apartment block, staring out across the darkness and lights and watching planes move slowly over the distance. Thorley would throw our empty Corona bottles whooping across the sky, see how far he could get them. Hear them burst and shatter far below us. He'd tell me he was aiming for the office building, the plane flying past, the cross on the church.

We'd play board games, match minds in tournaments of Connect Four out in the night air. We had an experiment going, testing which drugs impaired your Connect Four ability the most. Which ones enhanced it. I remember Thorley wrapped in his doona, wearing it like a snow jacket, his teeth chattering as he made his moves, all fucked up after taking something that didn't agree with him.

Uncle told us about a game he and his friend used to play, a game called Strangers. How it works is you pick a normal suburban house, and you study it. You steal their mail, get a list of who lives there, check out what they do for jobs, where they go. Watch them. The idea of Strangers is you have to learn as much as you can about them, so you can go into their house. The idea is you walk in the front door and pretend like you live there. Just go through, turn on the TV, grab a drink from the fridge, pretend like everything is normal. Be natural.

The research comes in when you are confronted, the occupants up in your face telling you to leave, to get the fuck out. This is when you need to have done as much research as possible, so you can respond: 'Bill, what are you doing? I don't understand. I live here.' This sort of thing fucks people up, their head hurts from the confusion.

The more information you have, the better this works. When you can refer to what they do, where they work, where they went for dinner last week. When you have all the answers it makes it harder for the people, makes them more confused. The idea of Strangers is to hold out for as long as you can, stay in the house for as long as possible, a second person outside with a timer running. The record, Uncle told us, is just over four hours.

Thorley and I kept watch on this one place for four weeks, hiding in the gardens and peeking through binoculars. Thorley had set himself the task of learning everything about them, a fucking perfectionist in his attention to detail. He'd gone through their rubbish looking for any scrap he could use. He'd watched crime shows, researched private investigators and their techniques, got into every detail of the game. This is how Thorley operated, very thorough, thinking of every speck of information. Re-thinking. Analysing.

Uncle taught us how to break into houses, what to look for. Loose windows, old door locks. Skylights are an easy option, as long as they are not too high up. Most skylights are only held in by an aluminium frame riveted to the roof. What you can do is bend the frame up and slide the skylight right out. Dressed in overalls and standing on a roof, no-one will suspect you are breaking into the house. They will assume the owners are aware of what you're doing. Who would be so stupid as to break in so obviously?

Bathroom windows are also an easy option. Normally the locks on bathroom windows are different to the others, less secure, as if the window being smaller lessens the chance of

147

someone trying to get in that way. French doors, Uncle told us, are also easy. Shake them till the locks come loose.

After a month, Thorley decided it was time to go in. We'd wandered through their house a few times, got the layout down, gone through their stuff. We knew everything about them. We waited for the husband and wife to come home, their cars pulled up along the street. Thorley looked at me, said: 'Four hours,' then walked across to the house. Me watching him through the binoculars as he grabbed the mail, flicking through it as he opened the front door. Disappeared inside.

The stopwatch reads thirty-four minutes and six seconds and Thorley comes out, runs across the road to me, smiling. He leads the way past me, running back through and into the park, along the path. It's late afternoon, the sun setting and shadows from the trees taking over all around. We run to the next main road, catch a taxi, get the driver to pull up at a bottle shop near the beach. Thorley buys a six-pack of Corona, hands me one, and we walk over to the sand.

The city beaches are not the same as the ones along the coast, the sand is harder, more polluted. No waves. Thorley and I sit down on the beach, watching the last of the daylight fade out. Watching the boats resting in the harbour or floating out over the water. A lone fisherman casting and winding under the street-light on the pier.

'You should have seen it,' Thorley tells me. 'Fucking, I go in and they are sitting on the couch in the front room, watching the news and I don't even look up, just walk straight through. The guy gets up in front of me quick, holds me back, says: "What the fuck are you doing?" and I pretend like I'm confused, upset at him, say: "Dave, what are *you* doing?" And the girl, Angela, she's just looking scared, standing up, moving towards the far corner of the room. Dave's like: "What are you doing?"

'And I tell him how I live with them, tell them what I know about what they've been doing and all that shit, use all the research. Dave's arm drops a bit, and he's got no idea what's happening, and the girl is screaming, like: "What's going on?" over and over. Dave's scratch-ing his head and I calm them both down, tell them what I know about their families and how I've known them for years and all that shit. I told her about her sister in Mexico – remember that postcard?'

Thorley smiles. 'And they're not buying it, but they're letting me sit on the couch. So after a while, I start acting like I'm offended by this whole thing, like I'm pissed off at them for ques-tioning me, and they get more confused, they don't know what to do. Dave says he's going to call his mate or something to ask them if they know me and I didn't have a good response for that.

'So, I get up, walk towards the toilet, then turn and run out the front door, Dave holding the fucking phone to his ear and Angela with her hands on her head. They were so fucking confused.'

Thorley drinks his beer. 'Bewildered,' he says. 'No idea how you could hold it up for four hours though, it's fucking tough.'

'It'd depend on the victims.'

'They're fucking lucky. I was gonna hit 'em with this.' And Thorley pulls out a loaded syringe, plastic cover over the needle, brings it up from the back of his pants. 'This would've fucked 'em up,' he says.

'What's in that?' I ask, forcing a laugh.

'I've gotta call Uncle, tell him about this.' Thorley takes out his phone, presses buttons, lighting up his face in the darkness.

'I thought you were against anything that had to be injected?' I say.

Thorley looks at me, phone pushed onto the side of his head, needle up in front of his eyes. He flicks the cover off with one hand, moves it around, looks at the sharp point from all angles.

'I am,' Thorley answers.

He jolts forward, stabs the needle my way, fakes like he's going to stick me with it and I recoil back hard. Thorley smiles, jams the shining tip into the hard sand, the syringe sticking out of the ground, shaking like a javelin. Thorley leans forward, touches his bottle against mine. 'We'll do this again, start with a new house.' And he smiles.

I look back behind us, back to the city, look up along the bay, the buildings lined around the coastline. The wind blowing my hair all over the place and making me squint when I face into it. Sand blowing up and against my skin. Cars flashing by.

'And they had Connect Four,' Thorley smiles. 'How cool are they?'

In that moment, before it all went to shit, everything was okay. Everything was good. Drinking beer on the beach and talking about Angela and Dave.

The sound of the ocean rolling in and out.

We get ready at Thorley's house, touching gel spikes into our hair before we tour the city clubs. The Saturday night bathroom beauty-salon routine. Alcohol, pants, T-shirt, drugs, shoes, alcohol, change shoes, check phone. Imagine this scene replicated a thousand times over in houses all across the suburbs. Young girls pulling their hair straight and painting on make-up and pushing their tits up. Looking over their shoulders in mirrors. Maybe tonight, they're thinking. Maybe tonight.

The city streets are lined with football fans, beanies and striped scarves, heading home after the game. Parents in dinner suits leaving restaurants arm in arm. Half-drunk teenagers kicking rubbish and yelling across the night. Blank-faced homeless people gathered by the train station. Police walking slowly past the darkened shopfronts, watching everything.

Thorley gives me tablets of something, tells me to take them. 'Post haste,' he tells me.

It kicks in fast and the night shifts to fast-forward, past endless club waiting-lines of bored punters and future alcoholics on every street. Vacant bouncers and door bitches chewing gum. Building queues at the fast-food restaurants, burgers wrapped in paper. Floating ice-blocks spilled across the pavement.

Thorley's eyes studying everything.

Uncle knows a guy so we skip the line at this one place, enter a darkened hallway, solid bass beats and people's voices echoing through the tunnel. The carpet sticks to my shoes and the bar is lit up in bright-orange neon lights. Girls in pigtails and singlets, glow-sticks around their necks. Guys straight from the gym wearing tight T-shirts. Yellow plastic wristbands. People sitting in darkened corners. Balding men nodding their heads to the beat but wishing it was still the early nineties. Some guy watching me from the corner of the room, maybe he's trying to pick me up, maybe he wants to kick my ass, who can tell? Strobe-lights flash like police cars at an accident scene or lightning every half-second, showing snapshots of Harris's eyes, lurking, searching for his target.

In between the flashes of colour and glances, pushing through gaps in the crowd, Aleesa is there, smiling and dancing with her friends, wearing a backless top, the smooth lines of her spine. She's seen me already, but continues dancing like she hasn't. Aleesa throws what's left of her drink into her throat, drops the glass to the wood of the dance floor, puts her arms up in the air, moves them as if she were fire in a game of charades.

I push through the dance floor crowd to get to her, rows of young girls and guys raping the air on elevated platforms. Aleesa rolls her eyes over to me, half-smiles. I ask her what she's doing here.

'What am I doing here?' she repeats, as if she were talking to as child. 'Is that your line?'

I tell her I don't have a line. I lean in to kiss her and when she pushes me back she feels stronger than she is. I can feel my blood cells fizzing inside my skull.

'The cells,' I tell her, bite at my lip. 'Sorry.'

'What are you sorry for?' she yells over the music.

'I'm sorry I never did tell you my name.'

'What makes you think I care?' Aleesa asks, smiling.

I rub at my forehead. For some reason it needs it. Her eyes shift away from me, to an athletic-looking guy making his way through the crowd. The athlete shuffles past me, his after-shave hanging in the air like a force-field around him. Aleesa puts a hand on his chest, takes a drink from him. The athlete is looking at her tits.

'This is Michael,' Aleesa says, gesturing to the athlete. Michael holds his hand out to me vacantly, gives me an 'I don't care who you are' look. Aleesa smiles with her mouth closed.

Michael's eyes move back to her tits and he wraps his arms round her waist, feigns dance moves so he can rub against her hip. Aleesa turns her head and kisses Michael, pulls on the hair at the back of his head and when she does this my heart feels choked up, coughing blood more than pumping it.

She keeps her eyes connected with mine as she kisses him, pushes her tongue into Michael's mouth, his hands moving down her back, resting on her ass. He pulls back from her mouth, starts kissing at her neck. Aleesa stares. Smiles. She stops him for a moment, leans close to my ear.

'Maybe you should go away,' she says.

I look at the athlete, narrow my eyes as I watch him swallow his beer. He moves his head to the beat, his eyes fixed on her ass.

'Go away,' Aleesa says. 'Or I'll tell them you raped me.'

I force my way back through the crowd and the stuttering lights and music. Away from them. People bumping at my shoulders, rocking me side to side. The air feels thick and it clogs in my throat. And when I look back the athlete has his crotch pushed up against Aleesa's hip, his face staring down at her body. Aleesa's eyes are calm. Still.

She knows what she has just done.

She waves, a cute up and down wave, as the crowd closes in around her.

Harris drops into the back seat of the car, drags the blonde girl behind him. She collapses onto the seat, too out of it to adjust her skirt as she goes. Up above the street a security camera watches from behind a tinted black bubble on a power pole. I notice cameras everywhere these days. Maybe that's the sign of a true criminal. Or a paranoid freak.

What happened is Harris decided on the blonde girl – I think it was the red singlet-top that did it for him – and she was with some gay guy who was up in her ear and eyeing us closely. Harris had hit her drink already when the gay guy pulled her to the strobe-lights of the dance floor. Green laser-lights that made me squint to see what was happening. Harris leaned in to speak to Uncle and Uncle leaned in to tell Thorley and the plan was set.

'You're Harris's second tonight,' Thorley yelled to me over the music. 'When he says, you go get the car.'

The blonde laughed as Harris gripped the top

of her arm and led her away. In the background, Uncle pushed the gay guy, held him back, put an arm around his body. The gay guy tried to get past Uncle, pushed at Uncle's arm. The gay guy yelled at Uncle's face, screamed over the music. Uncle stared straight ahead, blank-faced, pretended he was looking for something. The gay guy looking over Uncle's shoulder, struggling to get through. Uncle smiled, pretended to dance with him.

And the gay guy spat in Uncle's face. The gay guy looked like he couldn't believe what he'd just done, his weight shifting to his heels. Uncle flicked the saliva off his cheek, grabbed the gay guy's shirt with his other hand, crashed his fist into the guy's face, full-speed, right between the eyes. Even over the music you could hear it.

People cleared room on the floor for the gay guy to fall, his eyes wide open as his head rebounded off the footprints and spilt alcohol across the hard wood. He started convulsing or something too. Then the black shirts covering the backs of the two big security guards seemed to eclipse the entire crowd in front of me. And Harris yelled at me to get the fucking car.

The blonde has the expression of someone just out of surgery, distant, constantly trying to gather where she is, her eyes wide like she's struggling to focus. Harris props her up in the back seat, lifts her skirt up to the top of her hips, pulls her white underwear to her ankles. I can feel my blood cells moving, rolling through my veins. I rub at the back of my head when I think of the gay guy's skull bouncing off the nightclub floor. His eyes wide awake.

'Check her out,' Harris says to me, his fingers trembling along her pubic hair. He nods to me in the rear-view mirror, smiling like a kid breaking the rules.

He forces a finger inside her, looks to her face for a reaction. In my head, I'm thinking: *Fucken kids*. The blonde moans, sounds vague, like she's sleeping and moaning in her dream. Harris looks up through the windscreen, tells me to take a right towards the railway station car park.

A train whistles through, empty of passengers. I pull up under a streetlight, the orange filtering into the car, turn the engine off. Harris gathers up the blonde, fumbles with the door handle.

'Watch this, man.' He drags the blonde outside, letting in the night air.

'Hey,' I yell after him. 'Remember the rules, yeah?'

Harris nods, smiling, walks her to the front of the car, moving her body like a marionette. Harris lifts her top, pulls it off over her head, the breeze tingling goosebumps on her naked skin, her nipples hard. Harris bends her, lets her fall onto the bonnet, her tits squashed up against the metal. She's mumbling half-words and Harris's belt jingles, echoes around the empty white-line rectangles of the car park. He rips her skirt away, drops it into the night and I hit the steering wheel, open the door, lean my head out.

'You fucking idiot, the rules. How are we going to leave her as we found her now?' I yell to him. 'No evidence.'

'Chill out, man,' Harris says, not even looking up at me. I slam the door shut, grip my hands onto the steering wheel.

And for a moment, the blonde's eyes meet mine through the windscreen. Panicked. Half-aware. She looks down to see what is happening to her. She moves her eyes back to mine, then half-closes them. Her hair blowing up and across her face in the wind. Her head jolts up and down, rubs on the metal. Her dead eyes staring. Harris biting his lower lip and forcing his cock into her over and over.

And I lean closer to the windscreen, tilt my head sideways to look into her eyes, whisper to her unconscious face: 'You are looking at a monster.'

T roy calls me at 4:37 am, tells me he's fucked up big-time and I tell him to fuck off, hang up the phone. It rings again, whistling straight into my eardrum. Troy tells me he's serious, he's really fucked up.

'If you've hit another taxi driver,' I tell him. 'If there's not a dead taxi driver on the footpath when I get there,' I say, trying to gather the right words. 'Just fucking deal with it your – '

'She's in my room,' Troy whimpers back.

Like a caffeine hit, I'm awake. 'Who's in your room?'

'There's blood everywhere,' Troy says.

Like twenty-thousand volts through my body, I'm awake.

Troy is sobbing breaths down the phone line. 'I can taste . . .' Troy trails off, maybe he's crying.

'What the fuck have you done?'

'I can taste' – the phone's clicking, like he's gripping onto the receiver – 'bits of her brain, I think.'

160

The concrete roof of Thorley's building is bright white in the sunlight, too bright when I open the door from the stairwell, takes a second for my eyes to adjust. The roof is flat, with boosted square-shaped aluminium pipes, the kind people sneak around in in movies, all poking towards the sky. You can walk right across Thorley's roof, stand right up on the edge of the building, no security railing. Everything is dirty with pigeon shit and black soot from the city air that has settled over time and covered everything. People's fingerprints and shoe-tracks. One says Nike, clear as the day it was marked. This is the first time I've been on the roof in the daylight.

Thorley is sitting in his blue and white fold-out chair, wearing a big hooded jumper, his back to me. He's watching the office-workers in the city buildings go about their day under the dim lights. Each office looks like an open refrigerator door. Church towers and commission flats are scattered across the distance, the rooftops a patchwork of random colours. Buildings and billboards. Thorley is wearing big dark sunglasses and smoking, slumped in his seat. The wind brushes through my hair, chills through the fabric of my clothes. The buildings absorb the sound of the city.

Off in the distance is the ocean, the sail of a boat on the bay moving slowing towards the edge of the earth. I imagine some old greybeard fisherman, wearing gumboots and overalls, waving goodbye to society as the ocean carries him away.

The Connect Four set is dismantled, on its side, red and yellow pieces all over the place.

'If birds hear a gunshot they fucking leave.' Thorley doesn't turn to look at me when he speaks, lets his arm fall out to his side, holding on to his cigarette. 'They don't stick around to find out what's going on, there's no curiosity, no quickly heading home to get their shit. They get the hint of a threat and they're gone. Flocks of them covering the sky.'

Thorley takes a long drag, blows smoke across the clouds and sunlight. He arches around to look at me. 'Birds don't wait around to find out if they're fucked. When the humans come, they leave. No question.' He nods to me, like I get what he's saying.

'Sounds like the ocean,' I tell him.

'What?'

'The cars on the street below us, sounds like

162

the ocean, like water flowing.' I listen again, hear the waves of traffic. 'Like we're floating up here, a platform on the sea.'

'Maybe you should jump in,' Thorley smiles, tilts his head towards the edge of the roof. 'Seriously.'

Imagine hurtling free-fall down the side of the building, landing headfirst on the concrete of the footpath. I wonder how long it feels in the air. How much pain you feel when your body meets the earth, compacts and shatters like the paint tins they threw off the roof on *Letterman* one time.

'Did you talk to the girls?' Thorley asks.

'Yeah. One of them was Aleesa.'

'Aleesa who?'

'I don't know. She was at a party we had. The Susannah Lockshardt one.'

'Straight dark hair?' Thorley trails his fingers down from his head as if to signify this is where hair comes from.

'Yeah. Blonde streaks.'

Thorley does one big nod, pulls his bottom lip in. 'So she knows you, too.'

I nod.

'And you were able to make her listen?'

I say nothing, look out over the bay again, the sail boat.

'Did you let Troy talk to her?'

I nod slowly.

Thorley closes his eyes, puts his finger into

his mouth, pushes it around his teeth, touches his wet finger to his ear.

'The Samurai in Japan, one of the things they said was: When faced with a crisis, if you put spittle on your earlobe and exhale deeply through your nose – ' Thorley stops, exhales through his nose. 'Then, supposedly, you can overcome anything at hand.' Thorley squints into the sunlight, staring up from behind his shades. 'They have other things like that too.'

'So what do we do then?' I ask him.

He sits still, quiet. Waits for a moment. A car horn far below us.

'Maybe it takes a while to work,' Thorley says, snaps back to life.

I notice an Australian flag flapping in the wind, dangling from a construction crane in the distance.

'If she talks we are fucked,' Thorley says.

'She won't. Troy – '

'Troy is a moron. He's a fucking baby. If he gets busted for this he'll take us all down with him. The police just press him a little bit and he'll unload everything.' Thorley flicks his cigarette towards the roof edge.

Imagine Troy under police questioning, officers standing over him in a dark room, one bright light dangling from the roof. Tears dangling from his stupid eyes.

'Maybe Troy is our option then,' I say.

Thorley laughs under his breath.

'You wanna use this?' He holds out a black handgun, just pulls it up from his lap where he's been nursing it.

'Why do you have that?' I ask.

Thorley holds the gun with both hands, studies it. Doesn't answer my question. In his lap he has bullets, rolling and clinking in his over-sized jumper every time he moves. He smoothes his finger along the side of the trigger.

'What happens to us?' Thorley says, softer. 'Where is Troy now?'

'I dropped him at his house.'

I want to ask Thorley what he's thinking, what he's doing. You never can tell with him. Maybe the gun will be aimed at me next. Maybe this is where I will die, an imprint of my body among the footprints and finger-written names in the soot.

Thorley slumps back into his chair, cradles the pistol back into his lap. I watch him use his foot to make a smiley face in the black grime.

'I'm gonna go,' I tell him, turn, walk back towards the stairwell door.

'Hey,' Thorley yells after me, and I hear the peaceful jingle of bullets rolling together as he cranes round the chair to look at me. He has the gun lazily pointed in my direction, his finger caressing the trigger. 'Maybe you should jump,' he says, one eye closed so he can aim at me.

And maybe he plans to make me parade, pirate style, off the edge of this building. Walk the plank. Into the ocean. With the gun barrel looking at me, he holds all the cards.

'The humans are coming,' Thorley says, smiling.

And he makes a bang sound, whips the gun in the air, lifts it back to his shoulder.

M um calls, asks where I've been.
'Can't talk at the moment, Mum.'

Me walking along the footpath, pushing through the crowds of weekend tourists. Some sort of event on today, footpaths blocked in with orange plastic barriers.

'What's going on with you? The school has called your father. A couple of times.'

'I know Mum, I'm sorry. I'm doing okay, I've just had a couple of things on.'

'Your Nan is very sick. Your cousin is going to come and stay with us so we can all visit her. Will you please come home?'

'I can't at the moment, Mum. I'm busy.'

'Please? I almost forget what you look like.'

'Mum.'

And I can hear my frustration coming out. Stop walking, stand on the bridge overlooking the river, a group of rowers making their way along the water. Imagine Mum sitting around the house by herself, cleaning and re-cleaning things, waiting for someone to come home so she's not alone any more. Imagine Mum cleaning my room, making my bed, flattening the sheets out with her hands. Making it perfect for when I get back.

'I'm sorry, Mum,' I tell her.

And there's a pause. A silence on the line.

'It's okay, son. Please come home when you can.' Then silence again. 'I miss you.'

'Okay, Mum.'

'Okay?'

'Okay,' I tell her.

'Well, I'll talk to you soon. Be careful.'

'Okay, Mum.'

And I want to tell her I love her or something, but I don't. I want to tell her something has gone wrong, there's been an accident. Something bad has happened. But I don't. Just hang up, Mum still on the line, drop my phone back into my pocket. Keep walking towards the train station.

U ncle is driving someone's car. Not his. An old Volvo, one of the blocky, rectangle-shaped ones. He's jittery on the steering wheel, checking the rear-view mirror too often. We drive past a nightclub, lines of kids in their best clothes. High heels and make-up. We drive past dormant shops and neon lights. A police station, a strip club, a church. We stop at the corner, under a streetlight.

'What the fuck?' Uncle yells. 'What's going to happen now?' He gets out, leaves the door swinging across the street, runs over to the 7-Eleven.

The police called Uncle this morning, asked him about Troy. They asked Uncle about what he and Troy were doing at the Siam Nightclub on Sunday night. 'Who?' Uncle said. The police said they had been given information. To the cops on the phone Uncle said: 'Didn't even see him,' and the cops said they may need to talk to him.

'Where were you between – ' the officer started, and Uncle hung up.

Uncle comes back to the Volvo carrying cigarettes and bubblegum, throws them into my lap.

'Fuck him,' Uncle says. 'We'll fucking . . .' He trails off, driving back into the city night, cruising past the walls of buildings beside us.

'Aren't you scared?' he says.

I think for a moment about the consequences of my actions. I think of pain and blood and grinding teeth on the concrete. I think of years in prison, constantly fearing for my life. I tell him no.

'I'm at the end, man. One more thing, I'm in jail. This will fuck me.' Uncle is breathing heavy, jumps on the brakes as we approach a red light. 'Why aren't you worried? The cops have called,' Uncle says, turning his head from the road as he does.

I think of boiling water torture and tell him sometimes you have to pay. I think of being stabbed in my sleep and say: 'What the fuck have I got to look forward to? At least my life is interesting.'

Uncle puts his foot down, slides past the parked cars that line the road, comes too close to them. We flick against their side-mirrors, a thumping sound every time we hit, me pulling my head into my body and leaning into the centre of the car as we do. My right foot is pushing on the floor, as if hitting an imaginary brake pedal. Uncle looks deliberate, focused. He turns up the stereo, some bullshit skateboard rock music.

'What is this music?' I ask him.

Uncle looks at the stereo, runs a red light, car horns blaring then fading as we flash by.

'This is the new punk,' he says.

'New punk,' I say. 'Bullshit.'

Uncle yanks the handbrake on at the top of the street, sucks in air and it's like his heavy breaths are the engine of the car, humming and revving. Uncle stares out towards the train tracks, dozens of them stretching into the underground tunnels beneath Federation Square. They are dimly lit and heartbreaking. I imagine homeless people who've died down on those crossways and sleepers. From here you can see the glow hanging over the buildings, reflecting off the clouds. A halo over the city. With all the lights on it's never really night-time. A train slithers into the darkness. I remember going to this train station on a school excursion when I was a kid, learning about the historic building.

Uncle smiles, turns his head to me.

'We're fucked,' he says. 'What have we got to live for?'

'Normal life is too normal,' I tell him.

'Boring,' he says.

'Whose car is this?' I ask.

'Tomorrow we could be dead.'

'Yes. Tomorrow we could be. That is the worst that can happen to us.' I kick at the stereo with my heel, break it till it turns off. 'We are the New

Punk, not these bullshit fuckhead rich kids with guitars,' I tell him.

'Fuck what people think,' Uncle smiles at me. 'Fuck people.'

Uncle rips the car back to life, wrenches it back onto the road. He rams the accelerator, speeds down the empty straight past the Square.

'Get out now,' he tells me. 'I won't give you another chance.'

I pull the door handle and roll out onto the bitumen, feel my bones bounce off the hard surface. And lying on the road, I watch the car speed further away, headed for the train station entrance, the historic steps. It has preserved hand-railings and a concrete archway. A row of clocks that indicate the times of the next train to arrive on each line. Around twenty steps go up into the station.

Uncle's body falls out of the Volvo as it drives on without him, the engine no longer accelerating, just floating, idling towards the station. Uncle lies on the road, puts his head up to see the car jack up onto the stairs, crash into the concrete. A huge noise explodes through the city streets, resonates up into the darkness, off above the lights.

The twenty-four-hour people rush out of their fast-food stores and lonely bars to see the action. The car is embedded into the archway, bent metal bars and framework. Cracks running like veins up the concrete. The engine is still running. Imagine Herbie trying to catch the train with his human friends.

I run to Uncle, who's lying across the white lines of the road. He's laughing, slapping his hand on the concrete. He yells as I drag him to his feet, start running.

'The New Punk,' he yells. And I think I can hear tears in his voice. I think Uncle is crying.

'The New Punk,' he screams as sirens whine in the distance, echoing across the night.

The New Punk is not about guilt. I do not feel guilty. About the people I've hurt. The girls we've fucked up for future relationships. I don't sit up at night crying and hating myself. That's how they want you to feel. What you're taught to feel. All your life. You are trained to feel ashamed and hate yourself if you do bad things. It's what society relies on to feel safe. But guilt is fucking useless. Guilt is for people who think they can be forgiven. For good people. Because everyone wants to be a good person. Don't you want to be a good person?

People ruin their lives because of guilt. Fuck themselves up. Blow their brains out. Because of guilt. People stay in relationships they hate, work shitty jobs. Because of guilt. Fuck that. Fuck feeling guilty. Fuck feeling bad about what I've done.

The New Punk is about rejecting guilt. And I don't give a fuck if you're upset or angry. Do something about it if it will make you feel better. Or maybe you shouldn't sink to my level. Take a deep breath. There, you're the bigger person now, aren't you? Feel bigger? Now maybe you can sleep at night. I do not give a fuck about anything you do. Or say. Or feel. Feel bigger? Four stars for you. Now fuck off.

I refuse to feel guilt.

Note to psychologist: I do not feel guilty about what I have done.

I don't care if your fingers got broken. If your face got cut up. If your daughter got drugged and bashed and raped and left for dead in the street. What's done is done. I don't care if you hate me. I don't care. I don't care if you won't talk to me, if you want me to go away. Disappear. I don't fucking care. You think I need you? Fuck you. I'd love to see your face when this comes back around. I'd love to see your face staring up at me. And I won't fucking hold back. I won't feel bad for one second. I could tear your world apart.

You don't know what I'm capable of.

You fucking hate me?

Hate me.

Hate me, you fucking pussy.

Yes, I watched it happen. Just fucking sat there and watched her get fucked. Over and over again. I watched her vomit and bleed. She liked it. She smiled.

Hate me.

I don't fucking care.

I'd destroy another hundred people. Leave

175

them crying in the gutters with the rubbish and shit. I'd cut your face open without a second's hesitation. You think I give a shit about your world? Your fucking life? Put terrorist bombs on all the buses and trains, scatter body parts through the streets, tear down the buildings. I do not care. This is what you deserve. Let it rain blood through the streets and into the storm-water drains. Let it turn to anarchy and hatred and all-out war in the shopping centres. Fire bullets into the faces of the women and children. Blame them for this. Get back at them for this. I don't feel guilty about the world I am part of.

This is what we fucking are.

Fact: Everyone has someone who hates them.

I refuse to be a safe little nobody.

I refuse to be nailed down.

A name in the phone book.

A tax file number.

The New Punk is not about guilt. What's done is fucking done.

Troy never told me what happened to April. He cried and said he was sorry, but he could never bring himself to tell me how it happened. He became a shadow afterwards. Faded. It was much later when I actually found out about the incident, during the court trial when the details were read in horrific detail, me sitting in the wooden seats in the new suit my dad had bought for me, tears in his eyes as he straightened my tie. I remember playing with the sleeves which were too long, covered my hands to the knuckles. I remember trying not to make eye contact with anybody. Dreading more descriptions of how April had her whole life ahead of her.

They asked April's parents if they wanted to leave the courtroom before the details where discussed. The two of them sat close, bunched together, holding hands. April's mother clinging to a screwed-up tissue from her handbag. Through a gap in seats I could see their hands, gripped tight. I focused on their interlocked fingers.

And the details were read out loud.

From what I remember, it went like this:

'The events that led to the murder of April Bollen began at the Siam Nightclub in Melbourne. Troy Van Graas had been socialising with April Bollen and her friends Aleesa Desca and Bree Phillips,' a voice read, me not looking up, staying focused on those fingers, shaking. 'Both Desca and Phillips have given statements of their recollections of the night. All four were drinking alcohol and "were pretty drunk".

'At around three o'clock in the morning the group decided to leave. They split a cab, Phillips and Desca getting out at Desca's home, while Bollen and Van Graas remained in the taxi. Bollen told her friends she would be staying the night at Van Graas' home. Though both Desca and Phillips agree Bollen's judgement was impaired, they had met Van Graas before and had no concerns about their friend's safety, saying "he was a nice guy" and "had always been very considerate".'

Considerate. Each words sticking in my mind for a moment, processing slowly.

'Van Graas and Bollen arrived at Van Graas' home at around 3.20 am. Van Graas' parents were staying with family in Europe and he was living alone. Van Graas and Bollen went into his bedroom and sat on the bed. They listened to music and talked. Both Van Graas and Bollen continued drinking alcohol at the house.

'Van Graas says in his statement: "We were kissing and it started to get a bit full-on and I took her clothes off, then mine."

'Bollen was lying on Van Graas' bed wearing only her underwear when Van Graas took off his pants. He says: "She said she wanted me to get naked for her, to do a strip for her."

'Van Graas says Bollen then started laughing uncontrollably. He has refused to say why she started laughing.'

And someone coughed in the courtroom, made the voice stop for a moment, as if to give everyone a chance to take a breath. Thick air all around, sticking in my throat on the way down.

'Van Graas says he asked her to stop laughing, but she wouldn't. He says in his statement: "It made me feel upset and angry so I hit her. Not hard."

'Van Graas slapped Bollen across the face, trying to get her to stop laughing, but Bollen could not stop. "So then I hit her again, only with an open hand, but she just kept going. I kept saying 'Stop, stop laughing', but she wouldn't."

'At this point, Van Graas grabbed Bollen by the hair and pulled her close to his face, spoke forcefully, told her to stop. Bollen stopped laughing for a minute and told Van Graas he had hurt her. He says: "I felt better then, but I felt bad for pulling her hair, so I said I was sorry and kissed her head."'

And again the voice paused. Silence. Focus on their fingers. Locked together.

'Bollen then began laughing again, which made Van Graas "really upset". Van Graas grabbed Bollen by the hair, lifted her up off the bed then threw her onto the floor.

'Van Graas currently weighs one hundred and six kilograms to Bollen's sixty-one kilograms. The floor in Van Graas' room is polished hardwood. The coroner believes Bollen broke two ribs when hitting the floor and suffered deep tissue bruising around her right hip. Due to the alcohol, Bollen may not have been in pain at this point.

'Van Graas says: "I threw her down and she hit the floor pretty hard and I yelled, I said: 'Stop laughing, please stop laughing.'"

'Van Graas rolled Bollen back over so he could see her face as she lay on the floor. She continued her fits of laughter, covering her mouth with her hand. "I yelled at her again to stop and she was looking at me, right at my eyes, and she could hear me, but she wouldn't listen."

'Van Graas then stood over Bollen and stomped on her face. "I stepped . . . stomped on her face and she stopped laughing, but she was still smiling." He then stomped on her face another "twenty or thirty" times. Evidence indicates Van Graas used both feet in the attack, applying his full bodyweight to Bollen's skull. Van Graas describes "feeling her bones break". Van Graas has repeated several times to the interviewing officers that he could taste blood. "She made noises, like screaming with your teeth together."

'After the attack, which lasted around three minutes in total, Van Graas' bedroom was covered in blood. His clothes were spattered, his books on the nearby bookshelf, even the window, more than two metres from the attack, had Bollen's blood on it. Van Graas felt weak at the knees, like he couldn't stand up. He fell to the floor beside Bollen's body.

'"I asked her if she was all right and I shook her arm a bit. She didn't even really have a face. It was just blood and her curly brown hair. I could see her eyes, but they were both looking different directions. She was dead, and I knew that."'

Flashback to Troy's room, the 'Keep Out' sign on the door. The blood. Shut my eyes tight. Try to push the image out of my head.

'Van Graas has been using anabolic steroids to assist his muscle growth for some time, continuously upping his levels without medical consultation. Van Graas regularly spends thirteen hours a week in the gym or doing weights in his home. A statement from a friend of Van Graas reads: "Sometimes I've looked at him and thought 'Mate, you've gone too far', like his arm muscles are almost as big as most people's heads. If he hit you, you'd know about it." A personal trainer who has worked with Van

Graas says he was "like a giant. No-one would mess with him".

'Van Graas says he has suffered bouts of steroid rage before and that he cannot control himself when these bouts occur. Steroid rage is a documented side-effect of steroid abuse, though no direct links have been proven.

'The coroner reported that Bollen suffered severe skull fracture, with fragments of bone driven into her brain, resulting in her death.'

And after the final words were read out I remember someone crying, resonating off the walls of the otherwise silent courtroom. The interlocked fingers clutched tight and shaking.

'What did you feel when you saw April's body?' Dr Jessica Snowden asks. 'How did you feel about that?'

'What do you want me to say?'

'Just what you felt.'

'I thought it was a shame,' I tell her. Dr Jessica Snowden sits waiting, pen in hand, her chair directly in front of mine. Her feet pointed towards me. 'It was a shame, with that body, that I never got to fuck her.'

Dr Jess takes a deep breath, starts writing. What I know about Dr Jessica Snowden is she knows I say things just to push her buttons, to shock her. She knows I say things to test her, see if she can deflect them back at me.

'That's wrong, isn't it?' I ask.

'It's not right or wrong,' she says without looking up from her notepad, no emotion in her voice. 'It's how you feel, you can't help that.'

Dr Jess knows what I'm doing, she's seen this all before. Smart-arse teenagers and twenty-four-hour tough guys. Juvenile offenders who just don't give a fuck. Dr Jess has seen a lot worse than this. She stops writing, crosses one leg over the other. Taps her foot in the air.

In my head I remember everything. Every tiny detail. I remember Troy sitting on the footpath when Thorley and I arrived that night, hugging onto his legs. The dark patches all over the bottom of his pants like he'd been fishing at low tide. I knew it was blood, but in the darkness I tried to pretend like it was something else.

The door to Troy's bedroom had an old plastic sign that his parents probably bought him for Christmas when he was a kid. It said 'Troy's Room'. Underneath, you could see the outline from where someone had written 'Keep Out' in texta then someone had scrubbed it off. Troy unlocked the door and slowly opened it, as if someone were sleeping inside. He peeked around the door frame, both directions, then moved aside.

'Have you ever seen a dead person?' I ask Dr Jessica Snowden. She looks up, emotionless, bored. She's heard it all before. I lean towards her, get closer to her face.

'To see a dead person,' I tell her, 'to see where life had once been, their flesh now useless, it's not like reading about it. It's not like when you see it on TV. You can't imagine it, can't gauge it against anything else. You see yourself in that dead body. You feel how fragile you are.

I remember her chin was where it should be, but the rest of her head wasn't, it was caved in, squashed. Crushed blood and bone.

'Imagine taking your last breath,' I tell Dr Jessica Snowden. 'Imagine a boot stomping down on your face.' I hit my fist onto my other palm. 'Suddenly you can't breathe properly and the foot stomps again. Then your ears pop like they never have before, you can no longer hear. You go to say stop but the boot comes down again, this time on your teeth, cuts your tongue up as you try to form the word. It comes down again and your body is panicked but powerless. It comes down again. Your brain knows something is very wrong. Again. You will not recover from this. It comes down again and something breaks, pops, bursts inside your skull, you can feel blood on your skin but you can't taste anything. Everything hurts but is numb. You can barely make out where you are as it fades.

'And that boot just doesn't stop. Again. Again. Again.

'This is the end of your life,' I tell Dr Jess, staring her down, leaning right up onto the edge of my chair. 'This is everything you know coming to a halt right here, right now. Things you thought you'd see are gone. Your dreams, the assumption that you were special, that God has a grand plan for you, that something like this could never happen. You don't get to say goodbye. You don't get to touch the ones you love one last time. You're just gone. Your life can be over just like that.'

Dr Jessica Snowden maintains eye contact, refuses to look away.

'When I saw April's body, that's how I felt,' I tell her, clench my teeth. 'Is that what you want, Jess?' I swallow hard, lean back into my chair. 'Is that right?'

Dr Jessica Snowden has sympathy in her eyes, pity. She puts her pen and notepad onto her desk, uncrosses her legs, tilts her head slightly.

'It's okay,' she says. 'You've been through a very traumatic experience.'

And I realise I've just given her exactly what she wanted. She puts on that fake reassuring smile, nods to me, her hands rested onto her knees.

Dr Jessica Snowden.

You bitch.

You slut.

You cunt.

'Don't you fucking look at me that way.'

Someone belts at the door of Thorley's apart-ment and I'm awake, face-down on the couch, the TV still on. Cartoons means it's early morning. My elbow hurts when I let it drop, I can feel bruises and swelling from bouncing along the road. A bitumen burn on my leg.

Fact: There's no safe way to jump out of a moving vehicle.

Somebody belts at the door again, shaking the hinges and making Thorley's CD racks tremble. No-one ever knocks at Thorley's door. The way it works is there's a video identification system. The camera is down in the lobby. To get into the building you press the number of the apartment, the bell rings, the resident checks the camera to identify you, then buzzes you up, which opens the lower security door. Normally, Thorley leaves his apartment door open, waiting. But no-one ever knocks on the door just out of nowhere.

I yell to him, tell Thorley there's someone here and the door gets rammed again, harder this time, maybe because they heard my voice. Uncle runs in from the other bedroom, quickly pulling a T-shirt over his head.

'Who the fuck is that?' he says, panicked.

I tell him I don't know and the door rattles again.

'Open the fucking door,' a muffled voice yells from outside.

'Maybe it's the cops,' I say.

'No fucking way it's the cops. They wouldn't be belting at the door, they'd be saying "It's the police" and, you know, "We've got a warrant" or some shit.' Uncle is staring at the door, his hand in a fist. It's rammed again, the impact makes the windows creak. Uncle's eyes dart round the room.

He's saying: 'Why doesn't Thorley have one of those spy hole things on his door?' Saying: 'Doesn't Thorley have any weapons?'

'He had a gun yesterday,' I say.

'Where is it?'

'For the cops?'

'It's not the fucking cops,' Uncle snaps. 'Where's Thorley?' He runs to the next room.

'Open the fucking door now,' a voice says.

Another voice, quieter, says: 'We've got to get in there. We've gotta hurry this up.'

'It's the cops,' another voice yells.

Uncle runs back into the room, his eyes still searching.

'Where's Thorley?' he asks, looking around as if he's in here some place.

'He's not in his room?

'No. He let us in last night, didn't he?'

The door gets hit solid from outside. Then again.

'They're gonna knock it down,' I say. 'How did they get up here?'

'Who the fuck are they?' Uncle goes to the kitchen, stacks the knives from the drawer onto the bench.

The door gets rocked again, the paint around the hinges cracking and flaking onto the carpet.

'How do we get out of here?' Uncle screams, a carving knife at the ready. A CD rack falls to the floor as the door gets hit again. And again. And again. And my phone rings.

'Hello, this is Detective Senior – ' I hang up.

'Was that Thorley?' Uncle yells over the banging, getting more constant, the whole apartment moves as if it's shaking at the foundations.

'No. It was the police?'

'You're fucking dead,' a voice yells from the other side of the door. They've made a gap, a small opening at the top of the doorway, enough so we can hear their voices clearly. The hinges crack and bend with every hit. Uncle runs to the bedroom, runs back through to the other end of the apartment, comes back into the lounge room.

'What do we do?' he yells.

'You're all fucked,' a voice spits through the gap.

'Hurry up, they'll be here soon,' another voice says.

I tell Uncle: 'Open the door.' I push the magazines and empty bottles off the coffee table, the rules written in black across it, pick it up by the legs. I tell Uncle to grab whatever the fuck he can and get ready. The door jars again, enough room for them to put their fingers through.

Uncle puts knives into his pockets and grabs a metal stool, holds it up as he moves closer to the door. I hide myself around the corner of the wall, just by the entryway, wait for them to come.

'Hey,' Uncle says. 'The New Punk.'

I nod to him.

'Fuck them,' he says, a scowl on his face.

Uncle flicks the door lock from a distance, then flicks at it again and it clicks.

'Hey, fuckheads,' Uncle yells. 'The door's open.'

The door bursts open, the handle slammed into the wall and five, maybe six guys come tearing through. Big guys. Uncle swings the stool at them, hits one in the head. The guy puts his hands on his skull, stumbles backwards. Uncle throws a knife from his pocket but another guy quickly grabs his arm, then another punches him in the face.

I swing the coffee table as hard as I can at them, smash it directly over one guy's bald head. The words of the rules shatter and cut. I push it to make sure the glass goes into his skin. I swing the frame back again, push the broken, jagged glass still attached to the metal into another guy's chest.

'You mutherfuckers,' one guy says to Uncle, three of them have him on the ground. They're yelling Thorley's name. One of them says my name.

'This is what we do to rapists,' someone yells out. Someone hits me from behind with something hard and I swing what's left of the table frame around again, charge my way through to the doorway. Uncle is screaming on the floor.

What they are doing is bending his fingers back till they pop and break. One by one. I know this now. I hear Uncle screaming as I open the stairwell door and run down. I can still hear Uncle screaming as I run along the footpath outside.

And the police are driving in, lights and sirens, three cars rolling into the driveway. I only look back long enough to see the cops running from their cars and into the apartment block. One of them is looking at me, his radio up to his mouth.

And I run into the city.

H arris got arrested early in the morning, but here's the fucked-up thing. At around five in the morning Harris wakes up, hears a knock on his door. Harris gets up, half in a daze, trying to flatten his bed hair as he walks down the hallway, past his parents' room. They're still trying to sleep.

Harris opens the door and there's five guys standing there. One with a cricket bat. One with a wrench. Harris is wondering if he is dreaming this, if this is real. One of the guys says: 'You Harrison?' Harris nods like a moron and they grab him, drag him out of the house.

The fucked-up thing is this: Mr Craig Bollen runs a construction company. Bollen Construction is what it's called. You see it on trucks sometimes, on the side of cranes. Bollen Construction works on major projects and is a multi-million-dollar company. Craig Bollen made his way up through the ranks and has a strong relationship with the local union movement, attends rallies, helps fund campaigns.

But Craig Bollen is a broken man. Since his daughter was killed. She was taken home from a nightclub and murdered. Some guy stomped on her face. The face Craig Bollen had seen as a baby, had watched grow up. Craig Bollen is crying and trying to comfort his wife and two other daughters. Trying to find answers, to understand why his daughter was killed. And Bollen, he has to do something.

Craig Bollen goes to the police station to get the latest on the investigation. Bollen asks them to let him know who did it: 'Tell me his name.' The police know Bollen, they've dealt with him a few times before at rallies and protest marches. Bollen has always been co-operative and diplomatic. The police know him well and they talk to him. They tell him they've arrested Troy Van Graas for the murder and part of Craig Bollen is disappointed that Troy didn't get beat up for what he'd done. Part of Bollen desperately wants to cave Troy's face in.

'But,' the officer says, 'we have also been given information by a friend of April's, information about a group of young guys who may have also been involved.' The officer says maybe Bollen should talk to this girl, Aleesa Desca. 'Of course, we've never discussed this,' the officer says. Bollen nods, pats the officer on the shoulder.

Bollen uses his dead daughter's mobile phone to find Aleesa's number. Bollen knows who

Aleesa is, Aleesa and his daughter had known each other since primary school. Aleesa tells him about Rohypnol, about a rich kid named Thorley and his four friends. How they regularly go out at night looking for targets, girls to drug and take home. 'Rape squad' is what Aleesa calls it. She tells Craig Bollen about the parties at Thorley's house, the science teacher at school. Aleesa says everyone knows about it. Their rape squad. Aleesa tells Bollen how one of them even raped her one time.

Bollen writes a list of names, puts the paper into his pocket. Bollen calls around, gets a group of guys together, guys who can handle themselves, guys who get in fights with nightclub bouncers and win. One of them, he once got in a fight at the Casino and floored the first three security guards who tried to stop him. It took six to get him under control. These guys, they have anger in their fists. They pat Craig Bollen on the back, tell him they will take care of it.

Bollen talks to the police, he finds out when they are going to arrest the rest of this rape squad, where the police will go to get us. And Bollen organises a deal. A deal where he and his guys will get half an hour alone with these rapists, these monsters. Half an hour to 'talk' with them before the police arrive to arrest them.

The cop, he says that's fine, but no obvious signs of the attack. No bruises or cuts. No evidence. 'The media will be all over this one, we don't want people thinking the police might have beat them up.

'Maybe break their fingers,' the officer says. 'That's what the Iranians used to do when they were interrogating prisoners. What they'd do is bend the finger back to the point of resistance, then slowly pull it back further to drag the pain out. The Chinese actually impale people's hands with drill bits, but we don't want you to do that,' the cop tells him. 'Maybe pinch their fingertips with a pair of pliers. Or' – and the cop looks around to see if anyone is listening, leans in to Bollen – 'drop a lit cigarette in the kid's earhole.'

Craig Bollen and the cop shake hands.

And what they do is they get Harris onto the ground outside his house, these guys, and they sit on his back. One of them holds a hand over Harris's mouth so as not to wake his parents up. And they bend his fingers, one by one. Bend them back till his fingernails touch the back of his hand. They bend them back, then step on them.

They say: 'This is what we do to rapists. You target little girls, huh? Real tough, aren't you, buddy?'

And they kick and punch at his ribs. They flip Harris over, face-up, and Craig Bollen, tears in his eyes, he stands over Harris with the wrench. Bollen takes a deep breath, just staring at Harris's face. The other guys move back but keep Harris pinned to the grass.

'My daughter,' Bollen says, and he brings the wrench down onto Harris's knee, shatters the kneecap. Harris screams and cries and almost passes out from the pain. Bollen keeps going, belting at the bones, cutting a hole into Harris's striped pyjama pants. Harris's leg bending up the wrong way, more with each hit, his foot shaking, lifeless in the air.

The police arrive, lights but no sirens, and Bollen is still working Harris's knee, like he's trying to cut straight through it. The cops drag him off, get him to drop the wrench, clumped with blood and skin and dirt. The big guys move back, tyring not to look at Harris's leg but looking anyway, unable to resist the horror of it. The hand taken away from his mouth, Harris screams, cries out.

'I told you no obvious signs,' the cop says.

'Say he was trying to get away,' Bollen says, shaking the officers from his arms. 'And he tripped.'

Harris's parents rushing out, pushing past the cops.

Bollen's group get back into their car and head to Thorley's place. Bollen takes out his list of names, points to my name, says: 'This guy. This guy raped my daughter's friend.' The big guys crack their knuckles, grind their teeth. Bollen wipes dots of blood from his cheek with a handkerchief.

'This guy raped Aleesa,' Bollen says.

'**P**ull over, up at the park there,' Troy points, Aleesa in the back seat and wearing her school uniform, growling, yelling, screaming.

I pull the car into the gutter and Troy's already unclipping his seatbelt, looking all around, making sure no-one sees. I know what he wants to do to her. He stares at me as if asking for my permission. Aleesa is huffing, angry, her brown eyes burning beneath the edges of her fringe.

'What the fuck have you fucking idiots done?' she screams, leans forward, grabbing onto the headrest of Troy's seat, rocking it like a prisoner testing how firm the bars of the cell are. She grabs Troy's hair, pulls at the back of his head. The windows are fogging from all the yelling, uneasy breaths. Troy is staring at me, Aleesa grabbing at his white hair.

'Let me out of this fucking car,' she screams.

And Troy springs like a trap, grabs her throat, grabs it hard. Her hands shoot open, let go of his hair. Suddenly the car is silent, Aleesa making 'A' sounds deep in her throat. Troy's fingers pushing into her tanned neck, finding the space around her windpipe. Aleesa is choking, her body going into shutdown, her eyes staring straight up, mouth open. A tear rolls down her cheek.

I tell Troy to stop, punch at his arm to get him off her, then at his head. He loosens his grip, like fucking Darth Vader, and Aleesa sucks in air.

'You fucking idiot,' I say. 'You fucked this up in the first place, let me handle this.'

Troy takes in what I'm saying, says nothing in response. Aleesa is coughing in the back seat, hunched over herself.

I tell Troy to wait in the car, tell him he fucked this up. I'll take care of this. 'I'll fix your fucking mistake.'

Troy grabs my shoulder, his eyes moving all around my face, then lets me go. I pull at Aleesa, still sucking in air, pull her out of the car and into the park. The big fuck wipes a section of the window clear of fog, stares out as I lead her away.

'You fucking idiots. What have you done?' Aleesa is pulling away from me, swinging her school bag, slapping, pinching at my hands.

'Aleesa, just fucking keep walking.'

'What's happened to April? Do you know who she is?'

'No, I don't know who she is.'

'If anything happens to her you won't live to see next week.'

In my head I'm thinking: *Maybe that's not such a bad thing. Next week could be bad.* I look back to the car up by the road as we walk further away and into the gardens of the park, keep walking till we are out of Troy's view. Imagine his eyes turning red in the passenger seat. His teeth grinding.

Aleesa is staring me down, thinking of ways to hurt me.

'Aleesa you have to go,' I say.

'What the fuck are you talking about? What have you guys done?'

'Aleesa, just go, that way.' I point to the other side of the park, away from the car. 'You have to go now.'

'What's happened to April?' Aleesa snarls through her teeth, more tears gathered in her eyes.

I take a screwdriver out of my pocket. 'You see this?' I hold it up to her face. 'I was going to kill you with this.'

'So why don't you do it?' She stands firm. 'What's happened to April?'

'She's fucking dead,' I yell at her.

Aleesa looks like she's going to be sick, grabs at her stomach, like a kid just off a carnival ride, stumbles over her own feet for a moment. She's in pain, doubled over.

'And that guy in the car will kill you too if you don't run away from here right now.' Aleesa straightens up, gathers herself, rubs at her eyes.

And spits in my face.

'You fucking . . . You deserve to die. All you rape squad fucks. I'll make sure you all fucking pay.' She flicks her hair as she talks, leaves strands trailing across her cheeks, stuck to her lips.

'If you don't get out of here he will kill you, just to keep you quiet.'

'Who killed her? What happened?' Aleesa is crying, screaming at me.

'Aleesa, you have to go.'

'Why are you letting me go?'

I look at her face, her dark-brown eyes, tracks of tears across her make-up. Her lips.

'Just go, Aleesa,' I tell her.

She takes in quick, crying breaths, lets them out at once. 'Were you there when it happened?' she asks.

I tell her no, I wasn't.

Aleesa cries, her mouth sticking together as she speaks, her voice trembling. 'She was my best friend.'

In some place else, maybe now would be the time I would put my arms around her. Tell her everything will be all right. In some place else. In another life. She wipes at her face, then stands straight up, stares at me. Her lip trembling.

In another life.

She smiles to me, sort of, then turns, runs away through the park.

I watch her get further away, the lines of her school dress moving through the old trees and dead leaves. And when I turn around Troy is walking towards me, staring at me, his huge body. He's looking past me, scanning the distance.

'Where is she now?' he asks.

I walk past him quickly, back towards the car.

'What happened?' he says.

I'm trying to think quick. *She got away. I killed her.* Troy walks after me, dogging my heels back to the car.

'She won't be talking,' I tell him.

'Where did – '

I turn around quick, get right up in his face.

'She won't, fucking, be talking, you big fuck,' I yell, and in my pocket my fingers grip on to the screwdriver.

Troy stares. Imagine his rage kicking in right now, him tearing me up. Any second now. Troy looks back to the park, then to me, then stomps back to the car.

My hand is shaking, gripped tight on to the screwdriver handle. Feel it tapping against my leg.

It's funny how things are amplified when you know your life is over. Things that are normally in the background, sidenotes to your reality, they are pushed to the front. The smallest things become important. Like maybe you'll never see them again. Take it in while you can.

I walked the city streets all day, that last day, after running from Thorley's apartment. I wandered with no direction or reason. At first I thought about Uncle, his fingers bent and broken on the floor. Then about Thorley, and where he had gone. I thought about the fisherman on his sailboat, floating out and away. Maybe I should become a stowaway, get out of here. I thought of everything that went wrong. And just wandered. Watched the people crossing from corner to corner. A million lives passing by but never knowing each other. Car indicators flashing in time. A woman singing to herself. A man holding his wife's jacket, standing, waiting by a department store, a sad look on his face.

I visit the comic store, the toy store, the video

arcade, places that remind me of the time my dad brought me into the city. I stand outside the office where my mother used to work, feel the memories of my life. Those same sounds.

My mother who's sitting at home, waiting for me, jumping every time the front door opens.

The wind runs its fingers through the streets of the city, taking leaves from the trees and up to the penthouses and construction cranes that touch the sky. Down here below, we're at the bottom of the ocean. People clutch on to jackets and umbrellas as the wind gets louder through the canyon of buildings. Down here, we're like Atlantis to those on top of the skyscrapers.

With the grey clouds closing out the sunlight the shops look more homely, the first splashes of rain smudging across the warmth of the light inside. Loose flyers for concerts. People running for cover. The impatient traffic slows to parade speed. This is the uncomfortable symphony of the city in a storm. Raindrops on the car roofs. The ticking of the pedestrian crossing. Suddenly thunder. Suddenly a siren.

I wander the tiles of the Casino food court, watch a movie in an empty cinema.

This, I'm thinking, *could be the last time. Take it all in.*

It's raining heavy in front of the headlights of the taxi cabs. The city at night reminds me of sadness. The streets like a ghost town. Where there were hundreds of people in the daylight there is now only loneliness and distant strangers under the streetlights. Dormant construction cranes next to the skeletons of developments. Semitrailers that howl and scream unseen behind the buildings. The blue glow of a television in an apartment on the eighth floor.

The darkened alleyways awaken my childish fear of the night. Of monsters lurking.

And my phone rings, water all over the screen.

'This is Detective Senior Sergeant Davies.'

'What of it?' I say. 'Why do I care?'

'We want you to come in for questioning.'

'I accept that I have to pay for what I have done. I give up,' I say. 'Fuck you guys.' I talk like a drunk. 'You scanning my call?'

Detective Senior Sergeant Davies doesn't answer. I tell him I'm in the city. Come find me. I leave my phone on, the officer still talking in my pocket.

And I realise I have nothing to fear in the darkness, I have nothing to be afraid of.

It's me who is the monster. Lurking.

I decide to sit on a dripping park bench, in a deserted park, watch the skeletal trees sway in the building winds. And wait. Prey for lightning. Stare up at the white, grey clouds, moving across the darkness, covering the stars.

And there I am, smiling, rain-soaked to my bones.

There I am when the police find me.

My mother won't see me. She says I'm not the boy she knew.

> These animals have destroyed lives and
> degraded innocent young girls. They, in
> turn, should have their lives destroyed.
> S. Best, Coburg

The first night is on the concrete floor of a remand cell. Remand is what they call it when you're arrested and presumed guilty. In reality, it just means you're in jail. Harris and Uncle are there too, they sit in the corners nursing their broken bodies, bandages and medical tape all over. Harris's leg is wrapped up and held straight.

'I took a hit for you,' Uncle says.

Later, they bring in Troy, push him in with us, the officers standing guard outside, the security camera rolling. They do this to see if we'll unwittingly discuss what's happened. To see if we'll confess to more crimes, give them more details, make their jobs easier. I know this now.

Harris can't talk, he just cries and rubs at his face as best he can with his wrists, making high-pitched, defeated sounds. The only time he says anything is when someone walks past, then Harris yells, screams: 'You've made a mistake, you've made a mistake, you've made a mistake.' Chanting over and over like a strange mantra.

You've made a mistake.

You've made a mistake.

You've made a mistake.

Then he collapses back into a heap in the corner, holds his hands in front of his chest, wrist on top of wrist, to avoid more injury to his fingers. His fingers which are all bent out of shape and make me rub at my knuckles when I look at them.

Uncle is talking, but saying nothing. From the looks of it his jaw is broken, bulging out the side of his face. Every time he moves he winces and yells out. He tells me he took a hit for me, back at Thorley's apartment.

'And where the fuck is Thorley?' he mumbles. His voice sounds like his mouth is half-full of water. Like how you talk when you are brushing your teeth.

Troy stares out, like a gorilla in a zoo cage. A gorilla that has been humiliated, hurt, and that has now accepted its fate. He doesn't speak, even when I ask him what they've done to him. His giant body slumped, sort of piled on top of itself.

They take us out of the cell, one at a time. And when Troy and I are alone he says: 'I didn't say anything about you. I never said you did anything.'

'Don't know that it matters any more.'

'But I didn't,' Troy says. 'You would do the same for me.' He nods. Then he gets lifted to his feet, walked out along the linoleum hallway.

> I hope these boys get raped and beaten the
> way their victims did. They are a waste of
> space on the planet.
> *Concerned parent, Bentleigh*

A man comes into the prison cell, after the others have been taken out. I quickly stand up and without a word the man punches me in the stomach, so hard that my ears pop and my penis retracts. Then I've got that dry saliva taste in my mouth, my body going against itself, and I throw up all onto the floor. I fall to the ground beside my vomit, desperately sucking in air. Like a fish out of water. The smell getting deep into my lungs. The man laughs, then walks out. And the door is locked again.

> This is absolutely disgusting. It breaks my
> heart to think of the torture they have
> inflicted on innocent, defenceless girls.
> *C. Copeland, Greensborough*

And you know that good-cop-bad-cop routine the police always do in the movies? They actually do that. They call it the sweet and sour method. The sweet cop sits down with me, hands me a Coke, tells me about dumb criminals he has seen. He tells me about the guy who tried to siphon petrol from a campervan. The officer tells me how they arrived on scene and the guy was on his side, in the foetal position on the ground. This guy, he'd plugged his hose into the campervan's sewage tank by mistake. The officer tells me about would-be robbers who've screwed up, the guy who showed his license to the liquor store he was robbing to prove he was eighteen. The cop tells me these stories to make me feel like we're on the same team.

'We don't think you'll face the same charges as the rest of these guys,' the officer says. 'Maybe if you tell us what you know about the whole thing . . . '

'What whole thing?'

'You guys, going out, hitting the clubs.' The officer bobs his head to an imaginary beat when he says 'clubs'. 'What happens there?'

'Where?'

The officer leans back, looks disappointed in me.

The sour officer is a bigger guy than the sweet cop and he takes no shit. He storms in, stands over me, his hand in a fist.

'You guys go out and rape girls. What's the

problem? Can't pick up with your own looks? Your own personality? No-one goes for you nerdy private-school kids? Is that it? You little weakling. An ugly little shit who no-one gives a fuck about. And the girls don't want you, do they? So you have to force them to touch you, force them to open their legs for you. Does it make you feel tough to fuck an unconscious girl?'

This is the sour cop's job. To push and provoke, so maybe I'll break. His job is to get the details wrong in the hope I'll correct him.

'You're going to jail, and you are going to get fucked up in there,' the sour cop tells me. 'Do you know what they do to rapists? They'll cut your nuts off with a razor blade. You'll have no friends in there, among the murderers. They'll open you up just for something to do. Some of the guys in there, they're fathers too, they'll be thinking it could have been their teenage daughter you were fucking. They'll – '

'Pour boiling water on my cock, make it all melt together?' I say.

'That's just the start,' the sour officer says.

The cops push me into another room, a video player and TV on a trolley. One of the officers pushes me into the seat, the other presses play on the video. It's Susannah Lockshardt lying on Thorley's bed. It's Troy fucking her, Thorley poking his cock at her face. Susannah throwing up, Thorley shoving her face away. The video is shaky, amateur, moving all around, barely

210

letting you focus on what's actually happening. Troy holds his hand up in the air, one thumb up to the camera, smiling, fucking the unconscious body of a model. Susannah is making groaning, sick noises, moving very little. Then she stops dead, Troy still fucking her.

'You gonna fuck her?' Troy says, laughing. And the video stops, the screen rolling to some episode of some TV show. The officer stops the tape.

'You fucked her, didn't you?' the sour cop says. He smells of coffee and wears a dark suit. 'You had your turn next, didn't you? A defenceless girl, lying there, naked.' The cop waits for me to answer, narrows his eyes. 'It was you operating the camera, they've told us, then you pressed stop and you came over and fucked her too.'

I look at the chair beside me, the wood grain in the table, remember the sailor off on the horizon on the bay.

'Where did you get your drugs? Who helped you? Who else is involved?'

And I feel his spit on my lips and cheeks when he talks. I tell them Tom McQueen, Johnny Curtis. Ralph Newman, I tell them. Pronounced 'Raef', I say.

The sour officer leans in close to me, where no-one can hear. The sweet officer stands watching and the sour officer says: 'You and your friends, you're all going to pay.'

The officer pauses, as if waiting for me to react. 'I would love to squeeze your neck right now, feel the life drain out of your body. You're life is over,' the sour cop says.

> We need to make a stand against such
> extreme and inexcusable acts. Dispose of
> these monsters.
> J. Parsons, Eltham

The lawyer comes into the blank room, me sitting on one side of the table. Empty chair waiting on the other side. He says: 'Read this,' and drops a thick book onto the table. Then he leaves.

Out of sessions court. The room is silent and wooden. The smell of painted wood. The handcuffs pinch at my arm-hair. The judge looks pissed off already. Then we are led to the next cell.

> They do not deserve any mercy or leniency
> for the acts they have committed. No slap
> on the wrist. No second chances. They must
> be severely punished.
> J. Smith, Traralgon

And the next day we're front-page news. Headline stories.
Rape Squad Caught.
Gutless Teens Drugged, Raped Girls.
Monsters.

An officer throws a newspaper into the cell and I hear him say: 'They've got no friends now.' Underneath the headline, a photo of us being led into the police station, our faces pixelated, makes us look like characters from an eighties computer game. I'm thinking: *There's one for the scrapbook. One to show the grandkids.* They have photos of Thorley's apartment building, of Troy's street. Another headline, smaller, on page three says 'Stolen Car Crashes Into Flinders Street Station'. Says how they thought it was a terrorist attack, that maybe the car was loaded with explosives. And the letter-writers' page is devoted to us. Random names from across the state saying we deserve to die.

> Throw them to the rapists and murderers in prison, let them sort themselves out in there.
> *P. Murphy, Melton*

On their eighteenth birthday most teenagers are celebrating their first taste of freedom, getting their licence, drinking alcohol legally. On Troy's eighteenth birthday he was raped in a prison cell, his arms up behind his back, his face pushed up against the concrete wall. Some guy breathing stinking breath up against his skin, saying: 'This is what happens,' growling, deep bass sounds in his throat. 'You feel that? That is what you get for raping little girls. That is what you're going to get. Over and over.'

Then they pounded his head on the wall till you couldn't tell the tears from the blood streaming down his cheeks. Troy was raped and beaten and to stop the broken ribs and bruising he took to covering himself with his mattress in the corner of his cell, screaming and crying, hoping they wouldn't come visit him again. Hoping they won't have weapons this time. One time the prison guards foiled a plan to inject Troy with a needle infected with AIDS from another prisoner.

And without his steroids Troy Van Graas is shrinking, becoming normal-sized, his skin soft and loose from his deflated muscles, stretch marks on his arms. Apparently, he told his parents to never come see him. And he sits in his cell saying nothing. Just scratching at the walls and listening to the sounds of the prison. Other than in court, I haven't seen Troy since. Other than on TV, the news.

> These animals should have the same thing they did to these girls done to them, singled out and outnumbered.
> L. Roberts, Hawthorn

My mother says she didn't raise a monster.

In the blank room I read. I read about Rohypnol and the administering of drugs to enable sexual

214

penetration. I read about remand and police bail and the court process. This is my life. Honestly, for all the things you learn about law when you are arrested you should get prior learning credit for a legal course.

I read about psychology.

'The thing is,' the lawyer says. It's his saying, it's what he always says when he's about to make a point. If I ever make a speech about him – maybe at his fiftieth birthday or at his retire-ment party – if I ever do, 'the thing is' is what I'll open with. Everyone will laugh.

> They are the lowest level of scum. If this was my daughter I would hunt you down and make sure the punishment fitted the crime.
> G. Williams, Croydon

The reason the police called Uncle first is Thorley called in a favour. I know this now. Thorley and me, in Troy's house looking at the dead body of April Bollen, Thorley tells me to take Troy. Take Troy and talk to the other girls. Thorley says he'll take care of the body. Thorley wraps April Bollen in the doona from Troy's bed, rolls it up so he can carry it, carry her. Thorley calls Uncle, says he needs him to do something.

'You owe me big, don't forget that,' Thorley says.

Uncle arrives in a car, not his, an old Volvo. Uncle and Thorley put the body in the boot of the car, and by now it's daylight and a school bus drives by and both of them panic, but no-one seems to notice the blood. On the footpath in a tiny trail. On the doona. People going past on their morning jog, headphones and sweatbands.

Thorley gives Uncle cash and tells him what he should do. Uncle doesn't want to do it, but he knows he owes Thorley. And he drives off with the body stuffed into the Volvo.

Uncle drives to the half-finished house near the power station outside the city. This house has been half-finished for ten years. It has walls, a roof, but no insides. Up near the roof is a round hole where a skylight was set to go in. Maybe the owners ran out of money. Maybe they went to jail. Uncle drives the Volvo up to the house, out of sight from the road.

Uncle drags April Bollen's body out of the boot, unrolls the doona. He dry-retches when he sees her, covers his mouth, stands staring at her but not wanting to look.

Uncle picks at the blood and muscle where her face was, fishes for her teeth, uses a knife to cut them away, stabs at what's left of her gums to get them out. Thorley, he'd researched all the crime shows on TV, he knew what the cops would be looking for. 'Make sure you take all her teeth,' Thorley told Uncle. 'And her hands. No finger-prints, no dental records. No identifying marks. Dump her body in a hole, some place away from the city, dump her teeth and hands in a river or

216

a lake, but nowhere near where you leave the body.'

And Uncle, no idea how many teeth he's supposed to find, looks at the small gathering of them that he has created, like pebbles covered in blood. Checks and double-checks to make sure he has them all. Wipes his fingers on the doona.

Uncle opens the back door of the Volvo, takes out a new axe he has bought, price tags still dangling from it. Uncle chops at April Bollen's wrist, cuts through the muscle and bone and veins, splatters blood onto his face and clothes, and Uncle's thinking: 'I should have bought overalls, goggles.' Uncle puts his foot onto her arm to hold the bone steady, cuts through it, hits the concrete on the ground beneath.

He puts her severed hand next to the teeth then rushes outside to vomit into the long grass. Looks to make sure there are no cars around as he wipes at his mouth. From the unfinished house you can see right down to the intersection probably a kilometre away. On the other side is a new housing estate in development, the wooden bones of houses. Uncle picks up the axe, goes back in to continue. Throws her other hand next to the teeth. Stares at the faceless, handless body lying in the doona. Wet blood shining. Wraps her back up.

Uncle checks the street again, sees a police car turning in the distance. Coming his way. Uncle looks around the half-finished building,

April Bollen, the blood seeping through the fabric, staining onto the concrete. And the police are coming. Uncle drops the axe and jumps into the Volvo, shoves the accelerator to the floor.

As he drives off Uncle watches the police drive into the unfinished house. And Uncle slaps the steering wheel. He's thinking fingerprints, police records, identification. Uncle drives through the unfinished dream homes of the housing estate back into the city. Cursing and yelling all the way. Cleans the car, burns his clothes. Rubs the steering wheel til it's hot from the friction. Then he picks me up in the city and we drive.

Much later, Uncle is charged with perverting the course of justice. Accessory to murder. Uncle is charged for driving a stolen vehicle. Driving a stolen vehicle up the train station steps. Drugs charges. Assaults. Uncle, he's told his broken fingers will never properly heal, will always be bent out of shape. And in jail, he's just another fuck-up.

Much later, the value of the new dream homes on the housing estate drops after people hear about the dead body found up in the old un-finished house. The one up on the hill that looms over the entire estate.

Much later, Harris committed suicide in his jail cell. Harris, he was screaming, crying any time anyone could hear.

You've made a mistake.

You've made a mistake.

You've made a mistake.

Harris, first he swallows glass, then he cuts his own throat with a razor blade. Slashes back and forth hard and fast along his jugular vein, his windpipe. Apparently, this indicates he really wanted to die. Apparently, cutting your own throat is difficult because your carotid arteries are protected by your windpipe. Feel where your arteries are with your fingertips, feel the bumps and pipes you have to cut through.

Harris's mother now works for a teen suicide prevention group, gives talks to current affairs shows and high schools.

> Name and shame these cowards. They must
> be taught the consequences of their actions.
> Their parents should be ashamed.
> J. Locke, Essendon

My dad, sitting on the other side of the interview table, dressed in his best shirt, combed-down hair, he says: 'I don't know what to say to you any more.' Then he says: 'Son,' like he was going to leave that part out. My mother, she's asked my dad if maybe they can change their names. Get out of town.

'And maybe for my business,' Dad says. 'It won't look good for us.'

I tell him I understand.

Thorley is long gone. Apparently, he caught a plane out the night before the police arrested us. Apparently, Thorley was on his way to the airport when he let Uncle and me into the apartment that night. Thorley let us in, then snuck out as soon as he could, caught a plane to Europe. Or South America. And he is long gone. Or maybe that's just what I assume happened. Maybe that's what I've decided happened to him.

> That this can happen in our society is an
> outrage. These monsters should be deported
> to a country that still enforces the death
> penalty, along with their families.
> *J. Phelan, via e-mail*

My dad, he says maybe it's best if we keep our distance for a bit. Dad says everything will be paid for.

A tear slides out from behind his glasses.

'You've broken my heart,' he says. 'Son.'

'There's a ninth rule too,' Thorley says, tapping on his coffee table, his newly inked rules across it. 'The ninth rule is: "Always Have an Option."

'An option is someone you can pin it to. Always have someone, something in mind that you can shift blame onto. You never know when you might suddenly need money or a car or information. Or someone to point the finger at. Someone to get rid of, to keep quiet.

'An option could be a rich person you know who you can rob as a means of getting quick cash. An option could be someone who was there with you, someone you hate, and you can use their name and description if you get questioned. Maybe an option could be someone . . . ' Thorley rolls his hand in the air, as if looking for the right word ' . . . expendable. Always have an option in mind, as the very last resort.' Thorley nods. He notices my concern at this.

'When it comes down to it, we are not in this together,' Thorley says. 'We're not on the same team, we're not brothers. We are bad people. Bad people do bad things. Nothing personal,' he says.

'Why haven't you put that down on here?' I ask.

'I've run out of room on that, haven't I?' Thorley says. His thick black letters touching onto the edges of the glass. 'And maybe not everyone needs to know this rule.'

And maybe Thorley had plans for us all along. Maybe we were all his options, waiting to be used in one way or another. This occurs to me as the concrete holding cell starts to hurt my bones and I study the shadows of the bars across my legs, zebra style. Maybe Thorley had each of us for a reason.

He'd told me about Harris, keeping him around for money. He'd told me how Troy was losing it, how he was out of control and a fucking moron and a baby. But when he needed an enforcer, someone to go out and shut someone up, someone to threaten Aleesa, even worse maybe, he called on Troy. And Troy didn't want to do it, but he did. Thorley had them, he'd given them things, taken them places they'd have never got to by themselves. He'd given them girls, anyone they wanted. And everyone owed him for something.

Uncle scored drugs, was Thorley's connection to getting drugs. The reason they call him Uncle is one time when he was arrested Thorley came and bailed him out, paid cash, told the cops Uncle was his uncle. That's the real reason. Uncle told me this the last time I spoke to him. Uncle, leaning his forehead up on the bars of a cell, smiling, staring at the floor. His bent-up fingers.

Uncle told me how Thorley bailed him out and they partied into the night, drinking and getting fucked up and Thorley and Uncle kept the joke running all night.

'This here is my uncle.'

'Have you met my uncle?'

'Even my uncle is here tonight.'

They both played along and the name stuck. That's what really happened. That's the reason Uncle owed Thorley big-time, the reason Uncle would do anything to pay him back. If Thorley talked to the cops, clarified the truth with them, maybe invented a story about how Uncle intimidated him into doing it, Uncle would get locked away.

Uncle knew this.

Thorley knew this.

They all owed him for something.

We all owed him. But what did he have me for?

He'd helped me get back at Mr Arthur, he'd taken me out, given me drugs, a place to stay. But why would he want me around? What was his option with me? I couldn't think of any reason I held any value for him.

Maybe I kept him invisible. In the background. Maybe everything would look like it's my fault. The expelled fuck-up who everyone expected the worst from. Maybe I was his main option.

I think about this till the concrete is warm and I can ignore what's happening for long enough to sleep. Close my eyes. Flatten my hands on the solid floor, cold, bumps in the paint. Specks of blood which have stained. This is me. A fuck-up.

Cop comes past and stares in at me, and he stands in front of the light so I can't see his face, just darkness peering in. Stares for a long time, not moving. Voices somewhere down the hall. My skull rested on the uneven ground. I keep my eyes on him, afraid to even blink. This is what I deserve. I stay still, the concrete hurting my hips and shoulders. The cop leans in closer to the bars, almost rested onto them, looking closer at me. A big guy.

The cop walks away without a word, his shoes tapping back away from the cell.

Mr John Arthur came to visit me, waiting in a small grey room, patiently sitting, hands rested on a blank table. A beard covers his face now, but he still wears that same brown suit. He stands from his seat, shakes my hand. Smiles a satisfied smile.

'How are you?' Mr John Arthur asks.

'Why are you here?'

'I thought I might be able to help you, being a former teacher.'

'Why?'

Mr John Arthur looks either sincere or gleeful. In this blank room I can't really tell. He smiles a thin, lips-together smile, hiding behind his facial growth.

'My wife left me,' he says.

'You mean, uh, the chemistry teacher?'

'After those photos, after that we couldn't be the same.' He waits for my response. Mr John Arthur goes to speak, stops himself, then goes again. 'I always knew it was you.'

'What was?'

'I always knew it was you in the pictures.'

'What pictures?'

'Then when I heard about your arrest it just clarified everything. It all made sense. And I knew you did it.'

'I don't know – '

'You,' Mr John Arthur raises his voice, points at me. 'You drugged and raped my wife in a shitty hotel room.'

To this, I say nothing.

'She came home after work that day, the day I got the pictures. I heard her unlock and open the front door. She came in and I had the photos all across our white carpet, the carpet she wanted and was always so concerned with. "Don't walk on the carpet with your shoes on," she'd say.'

Mr John Arthur laughs as he replays the memory in his head.

'And I yelled at her, asked her to explain herself and when she couldn't I pushed her, shoved her shoulder. Just one time in our life together did I ever push her. She cried. She handed me a note she'd written for me that day. That's something we did. Wrote notes.'

Mr John Arthur reaches into his pocket, hands me a screwed-up piece of paper. It says:

> I love to hear your voice on the phone . . .
> I love when you tell me you love me.
> You are my life.

Away from the schools and students and sandwich lunches.
You are my everything.

'After she left I quit the school. I quit every-thing. Stayed at home watching western films, Clint Eastwood.' Mr John Arthur clenches his teeth. 'I locked her cat out of the house for days, refused to feed it. Every time it looked at me my wife rushed back into my mind, her voice, her smell. I wanted to be alone.'

He leans closer over the table between us. 'After I read about the case, I realised I had yelled at my wife for being a victim.' He stares me down. 'I know it was you. I want to hear you say it.'

Then it's silent between us. The blank room.

'What if I told you I came here today to kill you?' Mr John Arthur says.

In my head I'm thinking: *This does not surprise me one bit*.

'What if I came here today, spoke to the officers, told them I'm a former teacher. That maybe I can get through to him. He knows me. He respects me. And the police don't even pat me down on the way in. Why would they pat down a former teacher? A former teacher from one of the most prestigious private schools in the state. A former teacher who's just trying to help.'

Mr John Arthur is playing with something in his pocket. The room is empty, every noise reverberating in the corners. Something clicks.

'What if I said I've been planning this since the day my wife left, since my life ended?' Mr John Arthur suddenly looks unhinged, ready to break. 'I don't have anything to lose,' he says.

'Just say you did it,' he says.

I'm watching his hand in his pocket, thinking maybe an officer will come in, say 'time's up'. Maybe they are listening, ready to pounce on Mr John Arthur. Or maybe I'm about to have my brains splattered across the wall behind me.

'Just tell me you did it,' he says.

I'm thinking of the newspaper headlines, letter-writers.

'Say it was you.'

I'm thinking of my parents. My humiliated mother. My broken-hearted father.

'I just need to hear you say it.'

I'm thinking: *Bad people do bad things. Nothing personal.*

This is my worthless, wasted life.

And I say: 'Fuck you.' I lean in real close to the table, tense my muscles ready for Mr John Arthur to fire a bullet through my face. And I whisper: 'She liked it.'

Mr John Arthur closes his eyes, breathes hard and fast through his nose, as if I've just touched him with a burning hot iron.

'You fucking – ' Mr John Arthur spits words through his teeth, the veins in his forehead rising. He slaps his hand across his eyes, calms his breathing back down. Mr John Arthur takes his hand out of his pocket, clenched fist. No gun. He stares through his gloss-coat eyes. Looks like he hasn't slept for days.

'One day we'll meet again, then we'll see,' he says, stands up, squeals the chair over the floor as he does. He stares at me as he walks towards the door.

Mr John Arthur looks back, pain in his eyes, his hand on the door handle. I keep a straight face, my heart thumping like a door being kicked in. He moves like he's going to talk, then says nothing, opens the door to the noisy corridor.

And in the grey room it's silent. I look down at the heels of my hands, the purple indents where I've pushed my nails into the skin, clenched fists too tight.

And I breathe again.

T he New Punk is about me. I am six feet tall.
I am a man. An employee. A consumer. A
patient. A liar. A hypocrite. A drug-dealer. I am a
name on the police Serious Sex Offenders
Register. I am a criminal. A sexual predator. My
father's son. My mother's shame.

A monster.

No amount of good deeds can bring me back.

Some people are just bad people. Always
will be.

My life will not be about career prospects,
wife and kids. Sucking the boss's cock to get
ahead. Politics. Religion. Corporate ladder.
These things are fucking gone for me. I don't feel
guilty about the things I have done. About
Mrs Arthur. The woman in the car on the
freeway. The girl bent over the bonnet in the car
park. About April Bollen. I don't feel guilty for
the things I have done.

The New Punk is not about Thorley or the
rules or the fucking rape squad. These people are
not my friends. The New Punk is not about

them, their bullshit. We are not on the same team. We are bad people.

Fact: Bad people do bad things.

Nothing personal.

The New Punk is about me, I don't give a fuck what you think. I don't want sympathy. This is who I am. I accept everything that has happened. I will live the rest of my wasted life. There is no coming back for me, there is no white light on the other side. So fuck it. My perfect life is now and I will take whatever I want. You don't like it, then fuck you.

I am not interested in your respect or attention or compassion. I do not want anything from you. I will not apologise or cry or cut my wrists longways and lay down in a tub of warm water. Fuck you. It means nothing to me if you hate me. I don't give a fuck.

The New Punk is about me. And I will not tell Dr Jessica Snowden what she wants so she can shift me on to the next doctor who'll prescribe me medication, numb my fucking brain, sedate me into being what they want. A tax file number. A nothing. Fuck them. Fuck you all. I'm not going anywhere. I'm not changing my ways.

The New Punk is about my life. This is who I am. And if I ever let myself feel guilt I'll hate myself as much as you hate me. And my existence will sicken me. I'll become what you want. A worthless, hopeless, pill-popping depressive. Just like your parents. Just like you. Fuck that.

I am a bad person.
I am a monster.
And I hope you fucking choke.

'So have you figured out what's wrong with me?' I ask Dr Jessica Snowden.

'It's not about what's "wrong" with you,' Dr Jess says, and she does the bent-rabbit-ears thing with her fingers when she says 'wrong'. 'It's about helping you.' She writes notes, the paper reflected in her glasses.

'You know,' I tell her, 'I never did get the importance of saying hello to people, the importance of *me* saying hello to people when they walked in the room. Or goodbye either. I never got why people cared if I said hello when everyone else did. So I don't do it. I mean, if I'm the only person in the room I say hello, but if there's a group chorus of hello or goodbye any place I never join in. Same with singing "Happy Birthday" at a party. Why is that?'

'Sounds like social dysfunction.'

'That's it,' I yell, put one finger up high in the air. 'Socially dysfunctional. That's it. I have a social disorder. Dr Jessica Snowden, that is what is wrong with me. You have helped me. Thank you, I am now cured. We can cease the therapy.'

Dr Jessica Snowden stares, unimpressed by my celebration.

What I know about Dr Jessica Snowden is she knows I say things just to push her buttons. Like the time I told her I went home and masturbated about her after the first time we met.

What else I know about Dr Jessica Snowden is she lives by herself in a single-storey white house with a small brick fence and a simple, neat garden. Dr Jessica Snowden eats alone most nights, her and her two cats. She doesn't go out very often, prefers to stay home and read. Parks her car, a white BMW, in the street, wheels up close to the gutter.

'A social disorder,' Dr Jessica Snowden says, annoyed, me smiling back at her, my arms behind my head, as if my work here is done.

Arms behind your head probably means something.

What I know is Dr Jessica Snowden sleeps on the left side of her queen-size bed. She has one of those pillows that are hard but are supposed to straighten out your back. You see them on late night TV commercials. To get into Dr Jessica Snowden's house, all you have to do is push.

'So all your problems, everything you've done, you're suggesting it's all due to a social disorder.' Dr Jess flicks over my record, flips the pages in her lap.

To get in, all you have to do is push. She has

old aluminium-frame windows on her bathroom that slide sideways to open. To get in without a key, all you have to do is put pressure on the window, then slide it across. The pressure makes the latch inside useless as it only hooks over the frame. When you push, the latch is too far from the frame to hook onto anything. Then you're inside.

Dr Jess is writing notes quickly, aggressively, me reclining in my chair. My mouth wide fucking open, tongue feeling the ridges in my back teeth.

What I know is Dr Jessica Snowden's house is cold, lifeless, books laying all over the place, across the kitchen table. Her cats have tiny little silver name tags dangling from their necks that jingle when they run. Tiffany and Sylvester. Her bedroom is messy, but only three-day messy, clothes thrown around, underwear laying on the floor. She has no condoms in the bedside drawers. No dildo either. This makes me think she's getting fucked someplace else. Or she's hidden it. She has white sheets and the sunlight fills the room in the afternoon.

Dr Jessica Snowden looks at me, impatient.

'Social disorder,' she says.

And she's not beautiful, but she's not unattractive.

Dr Jessica Snowden has white sheets and when I laid down on them I thought about her naked skin touching against the fabric. Thought about fucking her.

'That's why you raped girls,' she says, deflects it back at me. Back and forth. We do this all the time.

'But you're wrong there,' I tell her.

'Where?' Dr Jessica Snowden asks, her forehead wrinkled. Anger.

And she's not beautiful, but most nights she's home alone.

And back in her office I say: 'I never raped anybody.'

A nd here's the thing: After all the court trials and police, the questioning. After newspaper headlines, letter-writers, phone-in polls. After Thorley, Rohypnol, private-school education. My father crying in disappointment, right there in front of me. After all this I'm free.

The thing is, I've never done anything.

I have never admitted.

Confessed.

Taken responsibility. For anything.

The thing is, I have never been charged.

I never raped anybody, never administered drugs to enable sexual penetration. I've never admitted to anything. Maybe I did smash a glass into the face of the big kahuna in Adelaide. But here's the thing, there is no record of the assault. No security footage. No big guy made contact with the police, no hospital reported treating him. So no charge. Maybe I left him scarred for life, but who's to say?

Maybe I did throw a bottle in the face of some derelict on a train, but there's no police report to prove this. Nothing.

No charge.

Maybe I did smash a glass table across the face of some construction worker in Thorley's apartment. But the police won't charge me for that because then they'd have to answer a whole lot of questions. Why were Bollen and his thugs there in the first place? How did they know where to go? What were they there to do? Five guys with weapons and angry stares, gritting their teeth, flexing their muscles. The police can never charge me for that.

Of course, I did know about Thorley, I saw what happened, but I've never confessed to anything. I watched these things happen and I did nothing to stop them. But maybe I was too scared to step up. Maybe I feared what might happen if I tried to stop them. Troy, prone to fits of rage. Thorley owned a gun. Maybe this was my option, my way out. Nothing personal, but these people, these criminals, they are not my brothers.

Maybe I told this story.

The car accident, the refrigeration truck, I've never heard anything about it. In all the interviews and investigations. Nothing. Stolen truck in a hit-and-run accident. Without specific dates, times, incident reports, they've never linked it back to me. So no charge.

And here's the thing, without being charged all they can do is make me attend therapy. All I have to do is talk to Dr Jessica 'Call Me Jess' Snowden two times a week, Mondays and Thursdays, so maybe she can get through to me, sort me out.

Because I've never confessed.

Admitted.

Been found guilty.

Even though they want to charge me. Even though they know I was involved, they just know I've done something, no solid evidence. Even after poking DNA sticks around my mouth and combing my pubic hair for traces of other people.

No charge.

Because I never did anything.

And the one thing they could charge me for, the one thing I did do that they could lock me away for, that thing has never come up. No-one has ever said anything about it. Not even me. That one night that only one other person would know anything about, there is one thing I did that would see me sharing a prison cell with Uncle and Troy. It's never come up, in all the charges, in all the investigation.

No charge.

Maybe if I think about it, think about all we caused. About Harris, bleeding from the neck on the cell floor. About my confused, isolated, devastated parents. Craig Bollen crying as he watches videos of his baby daughter. Mr John Arthur staring at his white carpet, the cat pawing at the window, begging to be allowed in from the rain. Troy, skinny and hopeless, the shadows of the prison bars on his face. Maybe if I think about it . . .

But I don't.

The fact is I am a bad person. Nothing will ever change that.

Where I am now, there is no reason for me to change. My parents won't acknowledge me. My friends are all gone. Here is my wasted life. Thorley's endless bank account gone.

Here is me with nothing.

Here is me with nothing to lose.

And because I was never charged you've never seen my face, it was never published in the newspapers, never aired on TV. I could be anyone. Some guy who serves you at the clothing store. That guy who smiles at you on the morning train. Someone you pass by everyday but will never meet. Who could say? You might even know me. Maybe you've seen me out some place. Maybe I've seen you.

Or maybe your friend. Your wife. Your daughter.

I could be watching her right now.

Dancing under the strobe lights.

I could be taking her home tonight.

Who could say?

This is me.

A bad person.

There is no going back for me. No forgiveness. Thorley taught me everything he knew.

And while you're there turning the pages safely
in your bed, your reading lamp across the words,
maybe I'm out in the night right now.
　　Who could say?

The Saturday night sounds flood the city streets. Thousands of young fuckheads yelling, screaming, laughing, trying to find some place to feel less alone. A group of young guys bully a homeless bum in the Bourke Street Mall. Drug-dealers and hopeless wasters shake hands at the Russell Street video arcade. People laughing, waving from the wound-down windows of taxi cabs. Skateboarders flipping and grinding along the concrete.

Under the streetlights it's never really night-time. It's just more uncertain. The shadows becoming monsters, lurking. Waiting.

The lines outside the clubs are building.

The sounds rising.

Groups of people with nothing to do and nowhere to go. But here.

I know a guy so I skip the line at this one place, the pulsing music getting louder as I come through the entrance, the crowd three-deep around the bar. Neon lights and cigarettes. A guy bumps past me and I feel the Stanley knife in my

243

pocket push against my hip. These days I always carry a weapon.

A smoke machine pumps clouds around the dance floor. And when it clears I see the one I want, a straw between her teeth, standing by a table. I move to the second floor so I can look down, watch her. She's not drinking alcohol, must have her keys on her. She smiles and her movie-star-white teeth glow under the neon lights.

The crowd is building, shoving, pushing. She takes her phone from her handbag, holds it to her ear, walks away from the music so she can speak. Away from her friends. I watch her leave the main room out to the corridor, a line of girls in short skirts and off-the-shoulder tops waiting for the toilets.

She yells into her phone, giving directions, says she'll see them soon. I get right up close to her as she speaks, moving with the tide of the crowd towards her. So close that I can smell her. So close that I could grab her. I clench my fist and listen to her voice, her head nodding as she speaks. The crowd around us, the bouncers standing up tall, the pulsing bass music. And I could grab her right now. I could hurt her.

I could tear her apart.

I move away as she turns back, still talking into her phone, her hand covering her other ear.

I crash through the door of the men's room, the smells of piss and alcohol and vomit. I crash through, push past some kid in a new shirt who smells of cheap deodorant. These days I don't stand aside for anyone. I ram the kid back against the wall. He doesn't do anything about it.

I walk to the nearest sink, rub cold water across my eyes, down my cheeks. My face in the mirror. My short hair. My dark-brown eyes that look almost black in this light. Dried splashes of whatever across the glass. I stare myself down, think about what I'm doing.

Some guy catches my eye in the mirror, stares at me. Just stands there looking. I drop my head, look down at my hands. They're shaking. Roll my fingers up, clench them tight as I can.

'This is my fucking mirror,' I say, look back at the glass.

But the guy doesn't listen, just stands there staring, looking at me. I turn quick and walk to him, hit the toe of my boot on his, my face up next to his cheek.

'This is my mirror. Fuck off.' I speak quiet, so only he can hear. 'I'll fucking cut you up.' My fingers slide along the metal of the Stanley knife.

The fuckhead says nothing, leans back away from me, puts his hands up as if to signal surrender. He laughs slightly, shakes his head, walks back out the toilet door and into the lights and crowd and music. And I go back to my mirror. Stare myself down. Think of her. Think of what I'm going to do.

She leaves with her friends and they wait

for a taxi in the cold night air. They are talking about where to go next, laughing and stumbling off their high heels. She sees them off, says she's heading home, and she walks across the street, away from the drunken rejects and hero bouncers. Car horns and conversations filter through the alleys and buildings.

She searches her bag for her parking-machine ticket as she walks, getting further away from the main streets, further from everybody else. And I get closer.

She stops walking to search her bag, rests it onto her leg. And I'm right up on her, my fingers crawling across the cold metal handle of the Stanley knife. So close I can smell her.

I haven't hit her drink. I haven't drugged her.

I want her to feel this.

The white clouds loom like ghosts against the night sky above us.

And right up next to her, my lips close to her dark tanned neck, the blonde streaks through her dark hair. My hand closing around the knife in my pocket. My muscles clenched. My heart faster.

Right up on her skin I speak.

'Aleesa,' I say.

Acknowledgements

Thank you to my parents and my family for their constant support. Thank you to Christos Tsiolkas for his knowledge, guidance and advice. I will be forever appreciative. Thanks to Jane Palfreyman for believing in my work and a huge thanks to Meredith Curnow and Julian Welch for applying their skills, abilities and intelligence to this novel. Thanks to Joanne Ipsen for always being there and to James Phelan for laughing at my jokes. This book would not have been possible without the involvement, each in different ways, of the following people: Simon Best, Wally DeBacker, Matthew Careri, Paul Murphy, Matt Brick, Paul Gratton, Rohini Sharma and all at Express Media.